P9-DNP-284

"That's it, doll. That's it." Marty's fiery words hissed in my ear. Her breath, ignited with quick, shallow pants, launched surging heat waves. I dug my nails into her back. I bit her shoulder, leaving dark red marks. Rock-hard, sweet Marty didn't flinch.

"Baby, whatcha doing?" Hurricane winds muffled Gina's words.

"Watching you," I gasped.

Marty lifted me from the table and pressed me against the wall. She tore open my blouse and tugged down my bra. Burning kisses seared my neck, my shoulder, the curve of my breast. Blood-flushed and thick, my nipples flared with desire.

"Is this what you want, doll?" Marty whispered.

She sucked the fever-pink tip of my breast into her mouth. An involuntary cry slipped from my lips.

"Who's with you?" Gina's voice's cut through the windstorm, cut through the thunder, cut through the sudden silence. I glanced at the cassette player — side one had finished playing.

Abruptly, Marty loosened her tight grip. Unpredictable as hell, she tossed me a dangerous smile and then, as though an afterthought, headed toward Gina.

"You got a problem, butch girl?"

Behind
Closed
Doors

ROBBI
SOMMERS

The Naiad Press, Inc.
1998

Copyright © 1993 by Robbi Sommers

All rights reserved. No part of this book may be reproduced or transmitted in any form or by any means, electronic or mechanical, including photocopying, without permission in writing from the publisher.

Printed in the United States of America on acid-free paper
First Edition
Second Printing, August 1994
Third Printing, March 1997

Edited by Christine Cassidy
Cover design by Pat Tong and Bonnie Liss
    (Phoenix Graphics)
Typeset by Sandi Stancil

Library of Congress Cataloging-in-Publication Data

Sommers, Robbi, 1950–
    Behind closed doors / by Robbi Sommers.
        p.   cm.
    ISBN 1-56280-039-6 (pbk.)
    1. Erotic stories, American.   2. Lesbians—Fiction.   I. Title.
PS3569.065335B44   1993
813'.54—dc20
                                                                        93-4756
                                                                        CIP

For T...

Because she opened doors
Took the time
Grabbed my hair
Came through windows
Broke the rules
Tracked me down
Sailed the seas
Raced the nights
Made risk easy
Watched me dance
Dressed me up
Loved me hard
And taught me how...

BOOKS BY ROBBI SOMMERS

Pleasures

Players

Kiss and Tell

Uncertain Companions

Behind Closed Doors

Personal Ads

Getting There

Between the Sheets (Audio Book)

Acknowledgments

Thank you for inspiration:
   The hands-on salesgirl
   the extra-hour escort
   the butch who played my scene
   my rebel-girl ex
   my bad-girl Sin
   the scent of leather
   the feel of Lace
   and my muse . . .

Author's Note

Within the context of fiction, I have not included safe sex practices between my characters. Crossing the line from fiction to reality, I strongly promote safe sex.

About the Author

Robbi Sommers was born in Cincinnati, Ohio in 1950. She lives in Northern California where she divides her time between Dental Hygiene, motherhood and writing. The author of the best-selling erotica *Pleasures, Players, Kiss and Tell, Uncertain Companions, Personal Ads* and *Getting There,* shyly admits to "liking a good time."

This book is a work of fiction. All locales are used fictitiously. Names, characters, and incidents are a product of the author's imagination, and any resemblance to actual events or persons, living or dead, is entirely coincidental.

CONTENTS

A MATTER OF TASTE

I wanted a look. I wanted a new me. Tired of my femme skirts, tired of lace, I climbed in my car and headed for my destiny. Must it be so difficult to mend a broken heart? To untangle one's soul from disillusion? I don't think so — not with a brand new Visa loaded with a four-thousand-dollar-limit.

Torlini's Menswear — not in the direction I usually drive, not on the way to *her* house — was hosted by a dark-skinned woman in a sleek Italian suit. Escorting me to notched-lapeled jackets and tailored shirts, she'd know the look, she'd show me the way.

"I want to get out of myself. I want a new me." The determination in my voice caught me off-guard. Sure you want out, sure you want to let go, my heart whispered. But so fast? Couldn't we just suffer the memories a year or two more?

I walked the aisle. My finger, like a desperate lover in a random mood, jumped from suit to suit. Maybe this, maybe that.

"This —" the saleswoman pulled a black suit from the rack — "is a very hot look. With your figure, your small waist . . ." She looked me up and down. "It's a thirty-eight, big I know, but there are things I can do to make it work."

Her raven eyes, shadowed with purple, twinkled. *Things she could do to make it work.* And my life? Were there things she could do with the suit to make *that* work? And my broken heart? And my fear that without Marjorie, I was no longer pretty, no longer witty, no longer anything? Yeah, let me see her make it work.

"Let's see." She ran her hands across my shoulders. "You're about my size, a little smaller in the shoulders." She moved in front of me. "I wear men's suits all the time. It's a great look, although not too many women can carry it off." She opened the dark blue sports coat she was wearing. "I cinch the waist with a wide belt, like this. Tightens the waist — thirty-eight is the smallest we carry — yet keeps the pants baggy. Hot look, huh?"

Hot all right, I thought, unable to ignore how her thick nipples teased the thin, white silk of her lacy camisole.

2

"Try it on," she said as she ushered me into a dressing room. "You can use my belt to get a feel for the look."

She unclasped her belt and the baggy pants slipped from her smooth waist to her curved hips. A hint of her white panties enticed me.

"Don't worry, it's just us girls." She giggled as though I feared for her modesty. "Johnny's up front with a customer."

"Just us girls," I said, feigning relief.

I averted my eyes from her slightly rounded belly, to her mocha-cream skin, and on to her seductive, frilly lingerie. A casual afternoon, the kind of day to be sharing a fitting room with a deliciously half-dressed saleswoman.

"Try on the pants," she coaxed. She stood in the doorway like a perfumed dark curtain. "And get that sweatshirt off. It ruins the look of the jacket. Just try it on with your bra. Jacket with no shirt, an interesting look in itself."

It's rare moments like this that I appreciate my straight appearance. A hetero woman — her pants dangling precariously on her hips, her fragrance ricocheting from the dressing room walls — had asked me to pull my shirt off.

"I *love* your bra. Is it satin?" She slid her finger along the edge of the cup and looked me in the eyes. "I just *love* satin."

My nipple hardened immediately but she didn't seem to notice. She handed me the pants and watched as I climbed out of my jeans.

"Matching panties. I'm the same way. I love nice lingerie. Just because *I* like the way satin and silk feel. I could care less about what the men prefer."

3

"Me too," I replied. Were we discussing lingerie or men?

"I like the way your panties fit. Is that elastic on the leg? I can't stand when the legs are binding." She pried her finger under the border lace and stretched gently. "God, they're great! Where'd you get them?"

I was distinctly aware of the circle of dampness now evident in the center of my panties. Want to see how the crotch fits? I thought wickedly. Want to slip that red-painted, well-manicured, heterosexual finger along *that* border?

"Victoria's Secret," I murmured nonchalantly. Unknowing straight women could be a hell of a good time.

Imagining what her smooth finger would feel like pressed in my fanciest silk folds, I stared absently into the mirror.

"Let's see the pants on," she interrupted.

Was her finger still in my panties? I thought so . . . but of course not.

I stepped into the suit pants. From behind, she grabbed for the waistband. Her hands were cool against my skin.

"Cinch the waist like this with the belt." She gathered the waistline, corralled it tightly with her wide patent leather belt and buckled it in the back. She flowered the excess material like petals around my waist then adjusted the extra folds around my ass.

"When they're baggy like this," she said matter-of-factly, running her hands along the slope of my ass, "the fit is a loose one. Even so, with a derriere like yours, it's hard not to still notice the

4

curve. See, I've got a flat ass." She turned, pulling her own pants tight against what I thought to be a nicely proportioned butt. "On me, baggy or tight makes no difference. But on you —"

Once again she cupped my rear. God, if Marjorie could see me now! Het-woman and I crammed in a dressing room. Soft, unassuming hands all over me. Should I feel guilty? Should I somehow advise my sales representative that I was a dyke and that her innocent, sweet hands were skating on thin, thin ice?

"Of course, we'd have to alter the length."

She was on her knees, turning up the pant cuff. I could see right down her heterosexual camisole. Her nipples, like fat chocolate chunks, stood pertly from each small breast.

"Do you like the way they look?" She motioned to the pant cuff.

My mouth watered as I studied her candy-treats. "Very, very much," I said whole-heartedly.

"We don't have to cuff them. Could do a straight look," she mumbled as she adjusted one pant leg down.

"*Not* straight," I replied, still smitten as her silk camisole caressed her toffee-budded breasts.

"I think you're right." She bent to cuff the pant and her distractingly loose pants partially exposed her lace-covered ass.

Nope. No question about it. She did not have a flat ass.

Still on her knees, she glanced into the mirror. "Do you like it like this?"

Oh sweetheart, how I like it is . . . Had I whispered or merely thought those words as I squatted next to her?

Her red, plush lips, only inches from mine, beckoned. I could press my mouth on hers, sink into the lush strawberry flesh, dive into her dark eyes that glimmered like small onyx ponds. Her perfume whipped like an approaching storm. Mirrors flanked the walls. From every corner her reflection surrounded me, enclosed me, penned me in. Next to me, across from me, she was everywhere.

"Are you okay?" Her pink tongue darted across her ripe, full lips.

I felt dizzy, lightheaded. She was over me, covering me, sweeping me into her fragrant cyclone. The tiny lace straps had slid from her shoulders and her brown, gumdrop nipples brushed accidentally against my face.

"Are you okay?" Her hands raced from my face to my neck.

The lights were twirling. Her pants were around her knees. She was leaning over me, loosening my belt. Her white laced panties, stretched tight across her lovely package, was remarkably close to my face.

I could smell her sex through the flimsy material. Persuasive and seductive — neither Gucci nor Yves St. Laurent could rival it — her expensive perfume seemed suddenly cheap and dreary juxtaposed to the alluring, spicy scent of her pussy.

I pulled her to my face and ripped her panties aside. Every het woman wants it this way at least once in their life — I know that. *We all know that.* The crystal dew, beaded and tangled in her secret hair, made this fundamental point pleasingly clear.

Her clitoris, a meaty molasses brown, poked magnificently between her thick-petaled lips. Like ruffled taffy, her small lower lips barely curtained

6

the spun-sugar slit. I pierced my tongue into the velvet darkness. Light licks, hurried flicks — I danced my tongue across her ridge.

So sweet — how long since I had tasted anything as sweet as she? My body ached for more. Had I eaten breakfast? Had I eaten dinner last night? When was the last time I had eaten since Marjorie broke my heart?

She was moaning. She was mine. With pointed tongue, I rolled circles around her slippery marble-shaped clit. *Nothing like that, huh, baby? Huh, baby?* No one knows a woman like another woman. Standard. Just yesterday, I had heard those very words on Oprah's talk show. *Nothing like that, right doll?*

"I've never felt anything like this before," she muttered.

"Good, baby, that's good to hear." My words slurred against her sopping flesh. *Tell me something I don't already know, straight lady.*

She squatted over my face. Her swollen pussy hung heavy and low. I separated her with both hands, sucked her entire clit-mound into my mouth while flirting my chin against her wide-open entrance.

I'd fuck her with my chin. I'd bury my finger up her ass. I'd milk her with my mouth until she creamed melted caramel down my face.

She lifted from my face to pull the tall, hinged mirrors close in around us. We were suddenly in a triangle of mirrored walls. Image after image after image of her squatting over my face — it went on forever.

I tilted my head back as far as I could and

slammed her down on my chin. The mirror to my right reflected the mirror behind her. I could see her heart-shaped ass sink onto my face. I pulled her cheeks apart. Her ass crevice was puffed like a miniature purple plum.

I'd fuck her with my chin. I'd bury my thumb into that shimmering plum pie. I'd do everything I could think of and more.

I lifted her above my face, spread her cheeks, and held her there. In the mirror, on and on, the glimmering pulpy entrance to her ass continued in hundreds and hundreds of far away images.

"Yeah, yeah." I poked my thumb against the puckered orifice. I pressed her down on my waiting chin.

Her cunt slid over me like a slippery, satin glove. Her ass sucked in my thumb. I could smell scents that would drive a lesser woman into a fuck frenzy. But I've been around. I'd hold my own. I'd do this straight lady right.

I greased into her ass. I took her with my chin. She rode me hard. She rode me sweet. I wiggled my thumb right up her. I pressed against her gripping walls. I held on hard as she rode into pleasure.

She was quiet when she came. Her body went rigid. Nothing moved, except her ass which pulsated tightly on my thumb. Demanding, grasping in fast, hard-rippled waves, her small passageway proved that she was pleased.

Thousands of images of us, on and on forever — there was no room for Marjorie, not anymore. That flickering heartache was losing its fuel. Nothing would get me now. I'd buy the suit. I'd eat dinner at the finest spot in town.

"I ... I ... I ..." my sales woman stuttered. Orgasm over, she had apparently plunged right back into heterosexual reality. (How convenient for them that it never hits when they're actually getting fucked.)

Pushing open the mirrors, she pulled on her pants, adjusted her jacket and ran her fingers through her curly dark hair. She glanced quickly at her watch. "Christ, it's almost five ..."

"It's really okay. Really," I offered sympathetically. She was embarrassed. Of course, she was embarrassed — mumbling as if it was the passing of time that had unnerved her so, as if her lesbian encounter was all in a day's work!

"You don't understand," she said nervously.

"Sure I do, really I do."

She wasn't paying attention. Instead she shoved my sweatshirt over my head.

"You go out first. If you want the suit — it looks great, really it does — Johnny will ring it up. It's half-off. After-Christmas sale. When I come out, just act real cool."

I felt guilty as shit. I hadn't meant to cause her such stress. Did she think someone would find out? Was she worried that her heterosexual identity would swirl down the drain from one quick, lesbian fuck?

I grabbed the suit, pushed through the dressing area doors toward the register. Johnny was ringing up his customer's purchase.

"Angie help you okay?" He shot me a quick look.

"Yeah, I want the suit," I said, careful to appear nonchalant.

"Be right with you." He turned back to his customer.

I glanced toward the dressing rooms. Angie hadn't come out. Was she back there crying? Was she shocked by what she had allowed me to do? Regret hovered around me like a thick rain cloud.

My thoughts were interrupted when the bell above the entrance door gave a short, sharp ring. In a black leather jacket, a Harley shirt, a pair of chaps that made my heart leap, a tough-looking, ass-kicking butch pushed into the store. She glanced at her watch.

"Angie just about through with her shift?" She motioned a hello to Johnny.

"Yeah, she should be out from the back any second."

The woman turned to me. "Nice suit. For you?"

I nodded, unable to speak, unable to look her in the eye. Son of a bitch, I had been had. A tinge of anger flickered then quickly snapped into amusement.

The butch smiled a cocky smile. "Let me guess. Angie helped, right? I know my woman's taste."

She knew her woman's taste? I ran my tongue across my lips and returned an even cockier smile. So did I.

SLEIGHT OF HAND

The ad in the gay and lesbian paper was small. Crammed in a tiny rectangle, sandwiched among the Personals, the single line inadvertently caught my eye. It was all uppercase, boxed by a thread-like black line — ESCORT SERVICE. DISCREET.

The advertisement, unremarkable as it was, held my interest only momentarily. It was the Personals, with their skillful deceptions, that attracted me. Promises of magical encounters, of meeting women and feeling suddenly transformed, intrigued me. Recently burdened by an annoying tendency to focus

11

on my flaws, feeling not quite pretty enough, I scanned the page, quickly surveying the offerings.

Once again, I was disappointed. Following last month's trend, this assemblage of fantasy-seekers had no sense of entrancement. What was the pay-off in meeting women who professed a desire to see the real me? They certainly offered no hope of liberation, no magic wands, no escape from myself.

My attention returned to that unobtrusive black-bordered box. DISCREET. The word was simple yet complex all at once. Fantasies, like mysterious shadows, slinked seductively between the letters. Women in dark, pinstriped men's suits would light my cigarette, would look deep into my eyes. With slicked-back hair, they'd whisper in my ear, sweet-talk me. Women who would do anything for money — on my arm, in my bed — anything I wanted.

Suddenly, I was engrossed in a mirage of limitless possibilities. Why waste my time with the disillusionment of the Personals when I could hire a woman adept in the skill of artful trickery?

I traced the flirtatious words lightly, then compulsively pressed my finger against the ad. A smudge of ink stained my fingertip and nothing more. What had I expected? That the hot little words would burn my finger?

I tossed the paper to the other end of the couch. If I could have it any way, how would I want it? She'd flatter me, charm me, convince me that I'm more than enough. She'd sweep me into a fantasy and carry me away. How provocative, how desirable, how enticing I would finally be! For a few dollars, she'd have me believing it all.

I reached for the paper and the phone in one quick movement. Why not? Why the hell not?

"Hello, this is Nadia. May I help you?"

The sultry voice on the other end of the line immediately unnerved me. Without warning, my heart began to pound, vigorously competing with my voice.

"I'd like to hire an escort," I blurted.

"That's easily arranged." Nadia's voice seemed sprinkled with hot spices. "Exactly what kind of an occasion did you have in mind?"

Had I made a mistake? Were these dates strictly aboveboard. The kaleidoscope of possibilities from only minutes before dimmed considerably.

"I thought we'd meet at my hotel," I said tentatively. The word *hotel* seemed to reverberate. "And just stay there for the evening."

There. I had said it. Would the phone be slammed down in my ear?

"And your specifications?" Nadia replied as though nothing extraordinary had transpired.

First a shudder of relief, then a tingling excitement, passed through me. My specifications? The world was suddenly a silver platter.

"She'd wear a dark suit," I said quickly. "And she'd slick back her short, dark hair." Is this how one did this sort of thing, like ordering a pizza?

"Does her height matter?"

I liked this — getting things exact beforehand. Why had I never considered an escort before? "Taller than five-six," I replied. "Not thin. On the butch side."

Why not have it all my way? A this-is-the-life feeling made me smile as I propped my feet on the coffee table.

"Most of the women who work for me are more on the femme side, although there is one woman —" Nadia paused momentarily. "Tell me a little more about what you're looking for."

Here goes, I thought, as if preparing to jump from a cliff to the ocean. Making a strong effort to defuse my embarrassment, I held my breath and dove in.

"I want her to want me." I focused on the vision of an aroused escort hungering to touch me. "In her eyes, her words, there will be no question that she wants me. I want a woman who knows what she wants ... and goes after it." My heart fluttered unmercifully.

"You want her to want you." Nadia's tone had a deep, provocative edge. "In other words, you want to be taken."

"Seduced," I said in a near whisper.

"Yes, seduced ..." Hot words, teasing words. "And then what?" Like slow-moving lava, her steamy words oozed from the phone.

I closed my eyes and visualized an unknown woman sweeping me into fantasy. "She'd be so crazy for me ..." I could imagine appreciative eyes flattering me, and a woman's mouth, dark-colored and plush, tantalizing me, ". . . that her desire would carry me away."

"Carry you away." Nadia's voice, low and suggestive, drifted down my neck, across my shoulder, to my raised nipples. So soft, so sweet, each word kissed me gently. "And take you where?" she murmured.

Her warm, wet words slid down my belly. I reached into my pants as if to capture them, to bring them back to my ear, but instead, my fingers found moisture and refused retreat.

"She takes the lead." My mouth felt dry as I spoke, yet my fingers were drenched in dampness. "She watches me, lures me. She goes after what she wants and what she wants is me."

"She's all over you without even touching you," Nadia said softly. "Her desire for you is what gets you high. Am I right?"

I wiggled my fingers between my generous folds of flesh. I was surprisingly swollen. "Yes."

"And when she takes you, will you want it soft?"

"Soft but certain." I fingered my thick sex.

"Like my voice," Nadia purred. "Soft and certain like my voice."

I wondered if Nadia's hands were as smooth and strong as her voice. I wondered if she was taller than I, stockier, less feminine.

"Her hands would explore me —"

"And her fingertips would be white heat." The words seemed to escape from Nadia's deep exhalation.

"White heat, yes." My own fingertips, as though charged with the image, churned across my enlarged

15

clitoris. Pressing, kneading, I drove the hotness against the hardened flesh. My heart raced.

"She asks you how you like it. She only wants to please you." Nadia's breath seemed shallow now, faster.

"She watches my body respond and sets her pace to that," I muttered as my slick finger pumped across my aching pulp. Eyes still closed, I saw colors: the room was hot pink, was deep rose, was wine purple. The white heat ripened to electric-red.

"So hot you melt," Nadia whispered. "So fucking hot you melt."

"Yeah, she makes me melt." Enveloped in sticky humidity, my fingers were lost in feminine tropics. "Yeah, yeah, yeah."

I strummed my finger around the fullness of my clit. It was Nadia, then the fantasy woman in the suit, then both of them holding me apart, whipping their fingers across my pussy.

"Montana." Nadia's sudden matter-of-factness cut into my pleasure.

"Montana?" My body was burning. This was not the time to stop. This was not the time to discuss vacation spots.

"Her name is Montana and she'd be perfect."

"Perhaps we should discuss my specific needs further before we rush into any particular —" My pussy ached. My clitoris throbbed. This was not a time to change the focus. Did I sound as though I was pleading? Could Nadia detect the begging in my voice? Thoughts darted desperately through my mind. I was incredibly close to orgasm. If only I could convince Nadia to take this conversation just a tiny bit further.

"Oh, there's no need. I'm an expert at this. Montana will be all that you could dream of. Her charge is one hundred and seventy-five per hour and — "

Nadia was speaking but I could barely decipher much past the one-seventy-five per hour. Who could afford such an extravagance? Not me.

Oh, but you will, my fired up body demanded.

"Visa or Mastercard?" I asked, beyond thinking.

"We take them both."

I sat in the lounge of the Carlton Hotel. Even with two shots of tequila under my belt, I was nervous as hell. Now that it was happening, now that there was no turning back, I was filled with sudden regret.

What if I wasn't attracted to her? Worse than that, what if she wasn't attracted to me? Three hundred and fifty dollars ought to make me look pretty damn good. Yeah, yeah, yeah, I hired her for two hours. I figured fifteen minutes for formalities, a half hour or so of seduction, forty-five minutes minimum of foreplay and some extra time in case I'm too nervous to relax.

I glanced in the mirror behind the bar. I looked okay, all things considered. I fluffed my hair and motioned for another shot. What the hell had I gotten myself into? The bartender smiled at the five-dollar tip and I downed the tequila. At this point what difference did five more bucks make?

The rest of the cash, stuffed in an envelope under the bed, was in the room upstairs. Do I give it to the escort before we started? After we finished? When you eat at a restaurant, you pay after the meal. When they deliver a pizza, you pay first. Was she a sit down or a delivery? I'd play it as it went.

If she asks for the money first, well, I'd hand it over. I brought four hundred dollars. Three-fifty for the two hours and a few bucks extra. I had a weird nightmare last night — the police had confiscated the agency's credit card records and my name was top of the list. *School Teacher Busted in Prostitution Crackdown* was tomorrow's front-page story. No thanks. I took a cash advance instead of bringing my card. If I don't take care of myself, who will?

It was seven fifty-five. Montana was due at eight. I moved to a table with a view of the registration desk. Any minute she'd approach the desk and ask for the envelope. My letter awaited her, with specific instructions. Would she read it fast and business-like? Or slowly, filled with intrigue? Nonetheless, once she read it, she'd come find me in the lounge.

Dressed in black, I had written. *Dressed in black and waiting for you.* I pulled a copy of the note from my pocket and reconsidered my words:

You'll see me in the lounge.
Dressed in black and waiting for you.
Come talk to me but take your time.
Do not talk about what we are doing.
Do not talk about this letter.
Look at me. Flatter me with your eyes.
Make me feel pretty, sexy, alluring.
Keep your voice low and suggestive.
Set the pace, it's up to you.

I like words. I like eyes.
I want to watch your mouth, your lips.
Let me see your hands, your fingers.
What can they do for me? Tell me.
You can touch my lips, my cheeks, my jawline.
You can sweet-talk me.
Do I tempt you? Let me know.
How much? Why?
Take the lead. Take control.
Go after what you want. You do want it,
*   don't you?*
Let me know how much.
Smoke a cigarette.
Devour me with your eyes
*   as you inhale, as you exhale.*
Take your time. Watch me, lure me, melt me,
*   make me ache for you.*
Convince me that you ache for me.
Then take my hand and lead me away.
Room 519.

Seven fifty-eight.

I wasn't asking for much, not when I was paying a hundred seventy-five an hour for it. Probably in the parking lot this very minute. Was she geared up, ready to take a stranger to the very limit? Walking toward the door, heading to the front desk —

Eight. On the nose. I wished I still smoked or had another shot of tequila. Leapfrogging butterflies bounced in my stomach. I could walk out now, go up to my room, turn on the television and lock the fucking door.

19

Leave her a note. Yeah, I'd leave her a note, slip a twenty in the envelope and never look back. I glanced at my watch, then scanned the registration area. Eight-oh-one and I needed a fucking cigarette. Not her. Not her. Her. Yes her. In a dark suit jacket and tight jeans, she walked up to the desk. She said something. She laughed. They handed her the envelope. My envelope. My envelope with my words. *Dressed in black and waiting for you.* Oh shit.

She ran her fingers through her slicked-back hair. One foot up, black pointed boot, she leaned against the wall as she opened the note. She smiled, a cocky smile, a confident smile, an I'm-going-to-please-somebody-good smile.

Dressed in black and waiting for you.

I could feel her eyes as she read the words. She hesitated, glanced toward the lounge, then back to the letter. My letter. My words. My demands.

I stared into my empty glass. I reread the matchbook cover six more times. Not looking up, I felt each step she took. One, then one more. The heat ricocheted around the room with each approaching step.

"Dressed in black and waiting for me?" Her voice was a deep half-whisper. She touched my face and a delicious chill raced through me.

My focus slowly drifted from the matchbook cover to her gray-steel eyes. Out of nowhere, the tequila rush suddenly kicked off, and I felt like warm putty. I wanted to speak, I wanted to make a cool impression.

"Yes," I managed. "Waiting for you."

She pulled up a chair. She sat across from me. Her eyes didn't waver, not once, from mine.

"I had no idea you'd be so —" Her smile was filled with promise, her eyes said one hundred sweet words.

"Are you pleased?" I blurted. Oh that's a *real* clever come back, I thought, irritated with myself. My tongue was as loose as my body felt.

"How could I not be pleased?" She laughed, her eyes glinting with amusement.

I felt as though I were slipping, like an oiled shadow, from my chair. Would she catch me if I slithered to the floor? Would she curl me in her arms and carry me to room five-nineteen?

Strong, well-manicured hands lit a match. She smoked. She looked me in the eyes. She was taking her time and like melting wax, I was slowly sliding to the floor.

"I like watching you. Your mouth —" Her eyes narrowed as she inhaled. "You're much different than I would have expected."

"And you're pleased?" Goddamnit, somebody needed to shut me up fast.

She pushed her cigarette into the ashtray and reached for my hand. "Let me show you just how pleased I am."

Magic and illusion are my best friends. One moment in a bar, a woman caressed me with heated words and conquering eyes. With a quick blink, we were someplace else. Sleight of hand, worth every cent. How we got to room five-nineteen, I'll never know. But we were there, on the balcony. Opera music soared from the radio.

Montana opened my blouse and pulled my lacy bra cup aside. The cool night air teased my nipples, coaxing them to thick pink points. As she touched my neck with tiny kisses, her fingertips, cool as the night, lightly squeezed the puckered, cherry tips.

Soft and plush, her warm lips pressed against my flesh. Hair scented like forest spice, cologne hinting of exotic mysteries — on my shoulders, down my breast, her tender lips left a trail of heat.

My nipples, hard and erect, ached for her mouth. I felt wet and slippery, as if my body oozed with thick, hot cream. Her fingers pinched. Her fingers teased.

"There's no one like you," Montana muttered between her kisses. Kisses that had shifted from gentle to determined. Hard against my breast, her mouth sucked, her mouth demanded.

"Really?" I asked. I felt suddenly on the verge of tears. Was I pretty enough? Did she really desire me or was the promise of money what made me so attractive?

I shook my head, as though trying to recapture my sense of self. At one hundred seventy-five an hour I should be approaching paradise, not close to tears. Perhaps the shots of tequila or the last four cigarette-less days had left me disoriented.

"Yes, really." The intensity in Montana's eyes threw me. "Really. Really. Really."

She enclosed me in her arms and wrapped me in her magic. From the darkness of the balcony — in a genie's spell, a magician's veil — we swirled to the bed.

She lifted my skirt, pulled my panties aside, kissing me still, enchanting me still. Montana sucked my breasts and belly, leaving purple-red brands all over my body.

"Yes, oh yes," I cried.

"So fine." Montana wiggled her fingers between my sex-soaked lips. "So very, very fine."

She sank her fingers deep inside me and pulled them out devastatingly slowly. "I want to feel it all. Every part of you." Her tone was demanding. Her eyes were hot steel.

I squirmed. I rotated my hips. The sudden desire for her to plunge back into me was overwhelming.

Her fingers, moist with sex, twisted against my vaginal border. She spread the wetness over my clitoris. Her strong hand, her firm hand, ran up and down my cunt. In the hair, across my swelling bud, over and over, she rubbed me down.

Two fingers at my cunt-slit pushed for entry. Two, then three, then four skirted the tiny portal. She never quite broke in, only pressed, pressed, pressed against the throbbing needy inlet.

"Grip for me, baby," she insisted.

I clamped as best I could. Her fingertips were on the rim. I pushed down attempting to take them in, suck them in, force them in. Montana unhurriedly stretched my opening with her fingers. She held me, then widened me until she pulled me remarkably taut.

She glanced up, her eyes steady with fire, and studied my body carefully. It was then that I realized that I was undressed. It was then that I realized that the lights were still on. I thought of my cellulite. I thought of my imperfect breasts.

"Turn off the lights," I said quickly. I reached for a blanket.

Montana grabbed my hand and held me firm. "Seeing you naked has me very hot," she said adamantly. "You are a beautiful woman. Please don't deny me my pleasure." Montana's eyes filled with indisputable passion. "Your hips, with those soft curves, are plush. An artist's dream." She ran her hand along my hips to my stomach.

"And your belly —" She nodded as though filled with ardent appreciation. "Luscious."

In the light, on top of the blanket, I looked down to my roundness. Luscious? Yeah, for three hundred-fifty, fat becomes plush.

"I like the way you look. I want to see you naked. I want to have you and watch every sweet moment."

I considered the lamp and the consequences of its intimidating light. There'd be no hiding. Montana would see it all. Never had I permitted a lover to keep the lights on.

"Shh," Montana said with a smile. "Stop thinking and start relaxing. Just this once."

I closed my eyes and hid in the shelter of my own darkness. Montana's breathing was deep, calming. Carefully, she squeezed my flaccid nipples until I felt them tighten.

"Nothing more beautiful than when a woman shows herself," Montana purred. "Nothing as beautiful as you in this moment."

Montana's words spilled over me like thick honey.

My body felt suddenly blanketed in warmth. Closeted behind closed eyes, intent on remaining in the dependable dark, I struggled to deflect the persistent light. My secure blackness, now shimmering with an illuminated border, wrestled with the lifting curtain.

She sees it all. She sees it all.

Eyes barely opened, I flirted with the light. At my side, with a smile on her face, Montana still sat.

"I've been waiting for your return," she said softly.

A small tear teased the corner of my eye. Montana captured it on her fingertip and held it to the light. "This is why you hired me, isn't it? To be seen once and for all?"

I shook my head vehemently and tiny tears sprinkled from my face.

"No?" Montana asked. "You don't want to be appreciated?"

Why was she saying these things? My instructions had clearly stated the rules.

"Don't talk to me about what we're doing," I demanded.

"You said take control and I am. How can I devour you, flatter you with my eyes, if you hide in the dark? I want you. Let me show you just how much."

Montana's hands slid over my breasts, across my belly, along my thighs. In the light, eyes wide open, I watched. She circled, then teased my nipples until they bunched into ruffled pinkness.

"Isn't that glorious?" she exclaimed. "And this, I like this."

Montana sucked fervently on my hardened pellet and then pulled up, her mouth still latched to my breast. She let the nipple snap from her lips. Dark-red and elongated, the nipple stood taut.

Persuading my legs to part, Montana slipped between them. She lightly nipped the flesh of my thighs. Hot moans, sensual moans, escaped from her with each quick bite.

A wild desire to spread myself completely, to show her everything, took over. I reached for my sex lips but Montana had already arrived, had already pulled me open. She was a woman who took control. I liked that. I craved that. Passion beat through me. Fire storms surged in my loins. *Watch me, lure me, make me melt.*

Montana pressed her fingers against my ripened entrance and massaged up and down the tiny door. Her tongue circled my vulva as her fingers tapped insistently.

"Oh baby, oh oh, baby," I muttered, watching every move Montana made.

She doodled her tongue across my straining clit. Lightly, quickly, deftly, she twiddled the swollen knot.

"Ready to melt?" Her voice had a desperate urgency. "Ready to show it all to me?"

"Yes. Yes. Yes!" I cried. I was ready. I'd show her anything. Put me on a stage, bathe me in a hundred spotlights, I didn't care!

She pulled my lips devastatingly apart and my clit jutted forward like a plump kernel. Her tongue returned to my pleasure point and flicked carelessly in rapid-fire short strokes. Fingers twisted hungrily at my dripping wet slit, dipped in, pulled out.

Sex-heat penetrated me like a drug. Every cell, every nerve-ending, shuddered with ongoing pleasure.

In the light, opened and exposed, I saw my breasts, full and beautiful, my belly round and beautiful, my thighs plush and beautiful. My body melted from an imperfect memory to plush, luscious and absolutely fine, fine, fine.

Caught up in a magician's spell, sleight of hand, skillful tricks — abracadabra, one-two-three, say the words and I'd be gone. Gone, gone, gone! I whirled, I flew high on a magic carpet then sank deep into rushing waves of thick, melted wax.

My eyes were opened, closed, opened.

"Oh God! Oh God! Oh God!" The room turned orange as I collapsed.

Quiet, eyes closed in the darkness, I managed to peek into the light. Montana was smiling.

"You're beautiful, all right," she whispered.

I smiled then glanced to the clock. Ten thirty. Overtime and out of cash. "We should stop," I said reluctantly.

Montana kissed me lightly on the cheek. "Gotta make a call."

As she reached for the phone, an immediate sadness swept over me. Sleight of hand, all right. Clock strikes twelve, the magic's over and I had turned into a pumpkin coach.

"Nadia, hi, it's Montana. Just checking in . . . yeah . . . I'm leaving now. See you later."

My heart fell to my belly — my large, bloated belly. I wrapped myself in the blanket and climbed out of bed.

"Where you sneaking off to?" She returned the phone to the nightstand and grabbed the blanket.

"I thought I'd get dressed now." I forced a smile. "Time's up."

"Just because I clock out doesn't mean I'm finished," Montana said as she tugged at the blanket. "I want more."

"You do?"

In a shower of magic dust, naked and in the light, I stood before her, suddenly unashamed. Feeling prettier than ever before, I let the blanket fall to the floor.

THE GIRL NEXT DOOR

There's a woman who lives in the building across
from me. If I stand on the toilet and angle myself
just so, I can see into her living room.

It started last Tuesday. Marvin said he wanted
the window cleaned. From the toilet, I could reach
the window. From the window, I could see her. She
was in a tight workout suit. Her hair was short.
Even so, she wore a blue bandanna around her
forehead. The bandanna matched her cropped
spandex top, her thick socks.

She was leaping around. Hands to the sky, hands

to the floor — she kicked, she bounced, she shimmied. An aura of unrestrained freedom soared around her as she danced and I wondered what music had caused such unmistakable inspiration. Within minutes, the small window was completely cleaned but I didn't move. Speculating about her choice of songs, I stood on the toilet seat and watched her.

Wednesday, the window was still clean. I climbed on the toilet anyway, just to make sure. She was sitting at her desk, talking on the phone. I couldn't tell what she was wearing, except that her top was black. I liked her in black. It suited her dark hair.

Had she already exercised today? It was noon. Perhaps she had a special time each day — yesterday, it was in the morning — or was she so busy that workouts had to be haphazardly squeezed into her life?

I peeked again at four. The living room was empty. Where was she? Out running errands? An extended lunch with friends? Without her, the room looked bare, inexplicably empty. I quickly shut the miniblinds and went back to "The Donohue Show." I didn't like the way the abandoned room made me feel.

That night, sometime after two, surging music woke me out of my dreams. Marvin, sound asleep, made snoring sounds not unlike a small bull, but otherwise the apartment was quiet.

Bladder full, I dragged myself to the bathroom. In the darkness, in the quiet, I thought of her. I knew it was late, that she was probably in bed, but I climbed on the toilet anyway. Her lights were off and the room was black.

Marvin left extra early Thursday morning. His important meeting meant he had to be at the airport by seven. I went straight to the kitchen. He likes when I have coffee and toast ready for him. The coffee should be hot and the butter slightly melted.

By five-thirty, he was out the door. From the bay window, I watched him climb in a taxi. I waved but I don't think he saw me. Nevertheless, I stood there long after the taxi left.

Six o'clock and the morning was still blanketed in gray shades from night. She was on the living room floor, face-up. A pair of white panties and a thin-strapped undershirt was all she wore. As I stared, transfixed by the vision of her pressed against the dark carpet, she raised her legs and separated them into a wide V. Wild tingling simmered in my belly and my heartbeat quickened.

Flustered, I stumbled down from the perch. What had gotten into me — peering from a window, invading a stranger's privacy? A thick uneasiness oozed through me. Was it voyeurism — blatant, sleazy voyeurism — that had driven me?

I hurried to the television and clicked it on. Benign interest and mere curiosity had led me to that window and nothing more. Exercise with Jake, one-two-three-four, one-two-three-four. I sat in front of the TV and watched Jake and his assistants work out. I laid on my back, I raised my legs.

A sharp image of her olive skin against the dark carpet shot before me. Her legs had been raised like mine now were, spread like mine. I pictured the pearly flash of white panties, tightly stretched across the thickness between her long legs. That same creamy tingling churned in my belly. What was it about her that fascinated me so? One-two-three-four, I scissored my legs in time to Jake's count. One-two-three-four. One-two-three-four. Apart, together. Apart, together.

Was she still on her floor? Was she also exercising with Jake — legs spread, legs together? She was my workout partner. Six in the morning, she and I, on the floor and all alone. One-two-three-four. One-two-three-four.

A light film of perspiration beaded on my chest. Was she also sweating or was I just out of shape? It had been so long, too long really, since I had had a friend like her. Someone to compare notes with, someone to pass the long days with.

Marvin, sports fan, had a great pair of binoculars. I was simply curious if she was sweating, that's all. In the bathroom, balanced on the toilet, I peered into her solitude. Head turned to the side, legs still in the air, she was waiting.

"One-two-three-four." I could hear Jake counting from my TV.

She moved her legs in time with his voice.

"One-two-three-four," I whispered. "One-two-three-four."

Marvin's binoculars brought her image to my face. She appeared so close that for the briefest moment, it seemed plausible to touch her tightened abdominal muscles. I focused on her straining belly and then slowly moved my point of concentration to her rounded hip. The white panty material rode high then curved toward her ass.

Down the hip to the thigh, I slid my focal point. One-two-three-four. She lifted and lowered both shapely legs together. One-two-three-four. One-two-three-four.

Flushed with impatient anticipation, yet uncertain why, I fervently hoped that Jake would review the leg scissors. I raced the binoculars to her face. Her head was still turned away. I scanned to her legs — one-two-three-four — steadily, she raised and lowered, raised and lowered.

"C'mon, Jake, give me the scissors," I muttered.

With quick, shallow breaths, I listened as Jake shouted instructions from my television.

"And lift-two-three-four. Lower-two-three-four."

My heart thumped recklessly. "Lift and separate, lift and separate," I pleaded, as if Jake would hear me and change his calls.

"And lift-two-three-four," Jake demanded. "And separate —"

"Yes!" I squealed. "Yes! Yes! Yes!"

I gripped the binoculars — no fucking way I wanted to drop those babies now — and breathlessly centered on the white swatch of panty material stretched taut between her sturdy, muscular legs.

She spread her legs slowly, one-two-three-four, and held them momentarily. Then together, one-two-three-four.

"C'mon, c'mon," I begged.

"Apart-two-three-four," Jake instructed. That-a-boy, Jake!

Zeroing in on the heart of her spread legs, I adjusted the dial, as if, perhaps, I could bring that remarkably tantalizing milk-white triangle further into focus. Yes, oh yes, I could see even clearer! A darkness, surely an area saturated with moisture, graced the center-point of her panties. Was that a slight depression, an area of indentation, beneath those cumbersome panties? Did she have a thick-rimmed slit beneath that soggy, soaked wet spot?

With my view, I stroked up her lovely body. Over her supple hips, across her streamlined tummy, I brought her undershirt-covered breasts into focus. Their tiny heads were reared up, as though well aware of my secret participation.

Jake had stopped counting. A commercial had taken his place. I slanted the binoculars in a sharp angle, back to the slice of panty between her legs. She was resting, knees dropped to each side.

What if she were to . . . what if on a wild fluke, she were to pull that panty crotch aside. For just a second, a quick, harmless second, what if . . . ? A quivering aching pounded between my legs.

And what if . . . what if she were to stir her finger . . . I shot my focus to her hand and centered on her thick, strong fingers. *. . . what if she were to stir her finger in her wet, wet pussy?*

Back to the soaked circle in her panties, then to her hands, then to her protruding nipples, I raced the binoculars. The throbbing in my own crotch felt divine. I jammed my fingers into my panties and twirled against my little, hardened nub of flesh. All the while, I caressed her with my demanding gaze.

Quick-shifting the binoculars from tits to cunt, over and over in fast circles, I fell victim to a delirious dizziness. My body, wild with desire for sweet abandonment, screamed for attention. My swollen nipples begged to be plucked. My clit hungered to be broken from its rock-hard shell.

I wanted to come, needed to come. One foot on each side of the open toilet bowl, I decided to forfeit the binoculars. Binoculars or not, window or not — extraneous props no longer mattered! Through the walls, I could see her. Eyes closed tight, I could see her still!

I bent low and spread my knees as far as possible. One hand held the toilet tank, the other fingered my throbbing clit. My legs were stretched, my muscles pulled tight. Delicious tension, hard and insistent, deepened in my thighs. My desire burst into roaring flames.

Legs strained, thighs rigid, I swirled my fingers in my sugar-cream sap. Through the walls, I could see her. She lay there, legs spread as wide as mine. Her peach-colored fingers had yanked that flimsy, wet panty crotch aside. Her pussy fur was dark as her black sweater had been yesterday. Yeah, I could remember how she sat at her desk, how she talked on the phone, as if oblivious to me, as if she didn't know! And all the while, nonchalant, she had flaunted her stuff right in my face.

Her mysteriously abundant hair couldn't hide her red-slit pussy. No binoculars, but I zoomed in anyway. She was swollen cherries — plump, meaty and ready to have the juice sucked right from the ripened source.

I pumped and tweaked my clit sack between my fingers. I dribbled the tiny round pellet with vigorous taps. And all the while, I licked her with my outstretched tongue. Yeah, I was so close that I could taste her, so close that I could smell her.

My face was in her crimson cunt. I could climb into her sex-soaked flesh and disappear forever.

Close, close, close, that close, that close to coming. Yeah, that close. Yeah, that close.

Sudden pressure in my bladder overthrew pounding sensations elsewhere. I had to pee and I had to pee now. I clamped down, I was too near my peak to break the climb. Inner muscles tight, I continued to steadily jerk my clit. Up and down, I drew the skin sheath over the bud.

The urge to pee intensified, but I squeezed my muscles even tighter. Strumming with my fingers, yanking my thin shaft, I held fast as I jacked my clit off.

Her legs were in the air, but held firmly together. I could see the thicket of black hair covering her bunched, fat lips, but nothing more. She was teasing the shit out of me but I didn't care. I'd reach right over, pull those long legs apart and plug her with my tongue. That's what I'd do, that's exactly what I'd do.

Nothing could stop me now. I let go of the toilet tank and cinched my pussy slit with my free hand. Balanced on the toilet seat, I tapped my clit and pinched my opening simultaneously. The heaviness in my bladder spiraled deep into my womb. The descending fullness, firm and insistent, launched a kaleidoscope of fiery pleasure.

Through the walls, she must have felt my feverish excitement, for she suddenly spread her legs and vividly displayed her showy snatch for me. She was deep purple, like overripe berries. I'd pluck that boasting little fruit right from the vine. I'd suck it in my mouth until I juiced it dry.

This last vision pushed me to the brink of ecstasy. I wavered as long as I could, a hard-riding cowgirl on an unbroken stallion, then leapt in. Golden heat spilled through me. In my belly, on my hands, the warmth cascaded in oncoming waves. The uncontainable pressure gushed out of me as I fell into complete release.

As though slipping in soft colors, I slowly straddled the toilet seat and rested my sweat-dampened face against the cool porcelain tank lid. I sat for long moments, drifting, until I realized that I was alone and could no longer see through the walls.

I pulled myself over to the mirror. Was she as lonely as I? As cool water splashed on my face, a sudden urge for one last look lured me back to the window.

Up the seat — *was she still there?* To the window — *waiting for me?* I peered through the once-abandoned binoculars. What I saw caught me so off guard that I almost fell into the toilet bowl.

Yeah. She was still there, all right. On the floor, panty crotch pulled to the side, the girl next door was waiting. With sultry eyes, and a come-get-me smile, she flashed me a neighborly wave.

DANCE OF THE SPIDER

Tonight, Beth Talbert, dressed in rhinestones and lace, drove to an East Bay bar and said her name was Pearl to any woman who asked. It was no accident that her black blouse emphasized the curve of her breasts nor that her leather pants fit snugly around her round ass. With jewelry that glittered like tiny strobe lights and red lipstick that begged to be smeared, Pearl owned any club she entered and any woman in it. She'd flirt with strangers, tease and tempt, just because she could.

"New in town, just passing through," she'd

whisper in a charcoal voice to whomever caught her fancy. "New in town and on my own."

Her panther eyes suggested predator and even the toughest women would find themselves inexplicably unnerved. Pearl, whose light touch on the bartender's hand seemed to snap like static electricity, was like no other that had ever walked into this East Bay bar.

A regular at the Stallion who thought she'd seen it all, Mattie's mouth fell open when Pearl made her entrance. Many women had come and gone through that worn, wooden door, but nothing had ever caught Mattie's attention like the woman in black.

With a hurricane walk that could knock women from their seats, the woman crossed the room and sat at the bar. The fit of her lace blouse said everything, yet revealed nothing. Her leather pants, tight around her curved ass, disappeared seductively into thigh-high boots. She motioned to the bartender and her bracelets glimmered in quick flashes. Like erratic fireflies in summer-night heat, sparkles flurried about her wrists.

Tucked in her corner, sipping her Scotch, Mattie — known to mind her own business most Saturday nights — watched vigilantly. Not unlike her stint in the Coast Guard, sitting in the dark, waiting for impending weather changes, Mattie studied the woman.

The woman swallowed her shot in one gulp and drifted to the dance floor like a wind-spun thundercloud. Before the full-length mirrors, seemingly lost in her silver-dream reflection, she wove a web of flickering mystery. Encircled in a spark-spun illusion, she swayed like a black widow spider who had no regrets.

As she turned, turbulent excitement bounced from the mirrored walls. A comet, a fiery planet, the edge of a volcano, the woman sizzled. Her torrential energy, frightening and compelling as an electrical storm, beckoned, teased, invited the onlookers into her intricate webwork.

Mattie knew about predators. With searing eyes that saw only in terms of survival, they stalked their victims and left them depleted. Mattie shook her head as if she'd seen enough, but could not shift her undeviating gaze. It's the dance of the spider that lures them in.

Under the strobe lights, Pearl danced. In the mirror, she could see a barrage of miniature rainbows drizzling from her rhinestones. The music surged through her like liquid heat. A slight bend, a whirl of the hips and she was saturated with pulsating rhythm.

Pearl was electricity. She shocked, she radiated, she connected if she chose. She could dazzle the darkness with a stream of crystal lights, intimidate the shadows with a twist of her twinkling wrists. There were no barriers, not for Pearl. The world was wide open and the night was hers.

The unrelenting beat sustained Pearl's voltage-high. Charged with power, she imagined hurling lightning bolts like Thor to the darkened

corners of the bar. Silhouettes of hidden women —
watching her? wanting her? — would be momentarily
framed in her light.

The dancing ignited as a mirrored ball lowered
and ceiling lights began to revolve. The haphazard
flashing spotlighted a corner table where a woman
sat, staring directly at Pearl.

Pearl's eyes met the woman's at the precise
second the lights illuminated her. For a brief instant,
the ebony woman was bathed with light. Then, just
as quickly, the shadows veiled her. Even so, Pearl
felt the woman's eyes burning from the darkness.

Does she want me? Pearl wondered. Does she see
that I'm a temptress — on my own and dressed to
dazzle?

Dressed to kill, Mattie thought as she watched
the woman's rhinestones shimmer under the
revolving lights. Leather pants and stiletto-heeled
boots . . . that kind of woman meant trouble.

Mattie pushed away from the table. The pool
table at the other end of the bar offered safety from
the web's unmistakable invitation.

"Want to dance?"

Mattie turned. Up close, the woman's red curly
hair and iceberg blue eyes were deadly. The spider
had Mattie cornered. I don't dance, Mattie thought
she'd say. "Sure, love to," was what came out.

"My name's Pearl." The luminous spider smiled
seductively.

You can lie in wait all you want. Mattie smirked
to herself. *One dance and I'm out of here.*

"I'm Kit." Mattie followed Pearl onto the dance floor. First lesson, never give a predator your real name.

"Kit. I like that."

The beat of the music slowed dramatically and the lights suddenly dimmed. It was a slow dance, a lover's dance, and Pearl turned to Mattie.

"Slow dance, okay?"

Mattie nodded and Pearl smiled. With a slow dance, perceptions change. Strangers touch, adversaries disarm. Pressed against the softness of Pearl's luscious body, lost in tidal waves of perfumed, copper-colored curls, Mattie closed her eyes and drifted out to sea.

On a shadowy dance floor, in a stranger's arms, Pearl drifted. This was when she was at her best — dancing with a stranger and on her own. The night was hers, all hers. She'd call the shots. The decisions would be hers. She could dance this woman into the corner. She could spin a web of desire so strong that the woman would have no choice but to want her.

Pearl felt the heat from Kit's breath in her ear. Yes. The night was hers, all right. They'd dance into the corner and disappear in the shadows. And then . . . and then . . . ? Pearl closed her eyes. And then . . .

As they danced toward the corner, Mattie knew she had willingly stumbled into the spider's lair. Siren hair, satin skin — there was no mystery how this spider had charmed her prey. One dance, Mattie reasoned, and then she was out of there. One simple, solitary dance.

As the song unraveled, Mattie imagined plum-purple silk streamers uncurling from the ceiling. Around her wrists and ankles, the ribbons wrapped, forcing her to fall victim. Almost certain she could feel the tension of sweet restriction, Mattie gave in. With a haphazard slip into the spider's web, Mattie was luxuriously out of control and wonderfully trapped.

Lost in illusions, she let Pearl push her against the mirrors. Hands and legs tied spread-eagle, Mattie was unable to help as Pearl unbuttoned her shirt and unzipped her jeans.

The dance floor was blissfully empty, or so it seemed. It was Mattie and Pearl and no one else. Tied to the mirrored walls, breasts exposed, pants jerked down, Mattie moaned with pleasure. And then . . .

And then, Pearl thought as they swayed to the music, once in the darkness, I'd have my way with her. I'd bind her with satin strips and tie her, spread-eagle, against this wall.

Pearl opened her eyes momentarily and imagined Kit pressed against the mirror, naked. An undulating wave of desire moved through her as she envisioned pulling Kit's arms above her head. Her pendulous breasts would be unrestricted and Pearl could do whatever she pleased with them.

As they danced, Pearl could easily feel Kit's

voluptuous breasts against her own. And how sweet, how very, very sweet they would look! She pictured large, brown areolas with hardened, dark, square nipples. She would pinch them, bite them, make them stand out.

Pearl suspected the thatch of cunt hair curtaining Kit's pussy would be incredibly thick. She'd have to spring the lips apart to see Kit's wine-colored treasures. But she would — oh yes — without a moment's hesitation, she would open those lips and expose that pouting hairless clump of flesh.

With her rosy-nailed fingers — her groping, talented, predatory fingers — she'd squeeze the hanging, fat clit. As if working a tiny udder, she'd milk the miniature teat, pull the flaccid burgundy hillock until it tightened like a stubborn, meaty clam.

Unable to be stopped, she'd tug and pulse the clustered wedge until Kit, helplessly bound but uncontrollably aroused, begged for release.

And she'd have me tied, Mattie thought as arousal climbed from the cleft between her legs, up her spine. And I'd never, not ever, want to be released. Against the wall, legs and arms spread, Pearl would fall to her knees and suck me dry.

A vivid image settled before Mattie's closed eyes. Perfumed Pearl, predatory Pearl, was on her knees. Her face was buried between Mattie's thighs.

"You like this, Kit?" Pearl murmured as she lapped. "You like the way I suck your clit?"

44

"Yeah, baby, yeah," Mattie moaned. "Suck it all. Take it all."

Pearl didn't answer. Instead she slid her ardent tongue into the peppery-scented sex pocket. Clitoris swollen, nipples erect, Mattie ached with delirious pleasure. She was wet, so wet that she heard slurping noises as Pearl's face slid up and down between her legs.

"Make me come, baby," Mattie begged. "Suck me dry, baby."

"Sure, yeah, sure, yeah." Pearl's words were muffled. "I'll suck you till there's nothing left. I'll pull you out of yourself till there's nothing left."

Pearl's tongue whipped across Mattie's ruffled-covered bud. In mock protest, Mattie struggled to free herself from the binding purple ribbons. She writhed and twisted but the resulting tightness around her wrists and ankles only served to spark her pleasure further.

With passion-filled acceptance, Mattie succumbed, now entirely at Pearl's mercy. Pearl wasted no time. With tongue to clit, she continued her pursuit. Again and again, she lashed then sucked.

Mattie slammed against the mirror as orgasm pounded through her. As though suspended by thin straps, she swung back and forth in the swirling lights. A prisoner, a captive of desire, she twirled in the spider's deadly web. The sharp, desperate vision caused Mattie's eyes to pop open. The beat had changed and the overhead blood-red lights flashed erratically.

*　*　*　*　*

The lights flashed as the music blasted into a fast beat. Kit had pulled away from Pearl with a fast thank-you-for-the-dance nod and an even faster exit toward the pool table. Pearl smiled as she watched Kit vanish into the crowd.

In a last look in the mirrors, Pearl saw herself disappearing. She hurried out the worn, wooden door, to the safety of her car.

Dressed in rhinestones and lace, Beth Talbert glanced in her rear view mirror but could no longer see Pearl. Even with red lip gloss and shiny rhinestone earrings, Pearl refused to return.

For a few entrancing minutes, Beth had had it all. With jewelry that glittered like tiny spotlights and red lipstick that begged to be smeared, she had flirted with strangers, teased and tempted, just because she could.

Suddenly feeling very tired, Beth started the car and headed home.

Mattie watched the black car pull out of the parking lot. She fought the urge to run after Pearl and ask for her phone number.

Lipstick and rhinestones and spider-web dreams, it was the dance of the spider and nothing more.

NO REGRETS

I hate heartbreak and the emptiness it spawns. I have a hard time sitting with it, a hard time getting through it, and thanks to Nancy, I'm stuck with it.

Nancy told me she "wants space." God, I despise that word. *Space,* the blanket word for *I want to fuck other women.* Who did she think she was kidding? Like I haven't been around the block, like I haven't said that very word to women myself.

Yeah, yeah, Nancy said it wasn't about other women. She swore to me on Alfie's life. Alfie, her cat of sixteen years, has no teeth, can barely walk and is soon to depart this world. If you ask me, Nancy wants a new kitten. If you ask me, Nancy's full of shit.

She wanted me to wait around, to "refrain from detrimental action." That's exactly what she called it, *detrimental action.* She sleeps with Willi and it's taking space. I sleep with someone and it's detrimental action.

A week before Nancy declared this sudden need for "space," I had the unnerving surprise of seeing her with Willi, tête à tête, at the Rockfield Café. They didn't see me. I could have passed their table with a marching band and they wouldn't have noticed. Space my ass.

As far as I'm concerned, she could have Willi (does that woman *always* wear that leather jacket?). I'm a free agent now. I can do what I want, with whomever I want, whenever the hell I please. I'd give Nancy her "space" all right.

I could have another girlfriend with the snap of my fingers — like that woman across the street waiting at the bus stop. Her streaky bleached-blonde hair tucked under a leather cap, her jeans cut out at the knees — whoa, check her out.

The message, *No Regrets,* was printed in black bold letters across her white T-shirt. Yeah, I liked that. With the nod of my head and a friendly smile, I could get her to cross the street and join me at my table. Perhaps a glass of white wine and an hour of small talk before heading back to her place?

Or maybe, I'd cross the street and catch the bus. Sitting several rows behind her, I'd take a trip to wherever she went. When she got off the bus, so would I. I'd follow her, find out where she lived and then return with a bottle of champagne and two crystal glasses.

Armed with a streetwise strut and a tough attitude that wouldn't quit, she sauntered to the corner phone booth. Forget the champagne, I'd bring a bottle of whiskey and we'd drink it straight from the bottle. We'd sit on her front steps and talk about queer politics.

After all, I'm pretty versatile. Just ask Nancy. She'd drag me to all her office parties and be amazed at how easily I'd fit right in with that stuffy group of C.P.A.'s. Ask her how much her parents liked me, or her daughter's school principal, or her reading group. Believe me, the list goes on.

So the punk lesbian across the street posed no problem for my social chameleon abilities. Within minutes we'd be on the same wavelength, I've just got that knack.

On her front porch, drinking whiskey, I'd make my moves. No, better yet, we'd stay on the bus. Maybe she'd be heading for Oregon and transferring to Greyhound downtown. Sure, a nice long ride out of state — strangers start talking, that sort of thing.

It would be getting dark and the bus would stop in a small town outside Eureka. I'd buy a bottle of whiskey in the small grocery. Behind me in line, she'd be buying a pack of smokes.

Only five minutes until departure, she's leaning against an outside pole and smoking a cigarette.

"Where you headed?" I asked.

"Eugene."

Not bothering to look toward me, she stared out at the starry night sky.

"Me too." I offered as if she had asked.

"Oh yeah?" She shot me a quick up-and-down appraisal.

"Long ride, huh?" I studied the tiny gold hoop in her nose.

Willi had her nose pierced. How can someone hold a credible conversation with a pierced person and not stare at the extra hole in her nose? Whenever I'd talk to Willi, I'd always flash on the image of her blowing her nose with one finger over the little hole. Hard for me to take that type seriously, although it seems Nancy doesn't have that sort of problem with the nose thing.

"Yeah, pretty boring ride." She tossed the cigarette butt to the ground.

"Want to kill some time?" I opened my leather jacket to reveal the bottle of whiskey in my inner pocket.

Okay, so I've got a leather jacket on, big deal. Just because Willi wears one every goddamned day of her life, just because Willi's moving in on my girl, doesn't mean I'm imitating her style. So Nancy's taking space with that type of woman, that doesn't mean I'm going be making changes to suit her frivolous fancy. I'm wearing the leather jacket because I'm trying to make this punk-dyke. The jacket goes with the territory, that's all.

So we're on the bus, sitting side by side in the dark, passing the bottle back and forth. She guzzled the whiskey like apple juice while I silently congratulated myself for my remarkable insight. Just one look at a person and I get a general feeling about what they like.

Except for Nancy. Nancy was a different story all together. Who could figure what she wanted at this point? Out of nowhere, she proclaimed her need for space. Space. I suppose that's what attracted her to Willi — the vast space between Willi's ears. Leather jacket and eccentric look does not a conversation make.

"I'm ripped," Johnson giggled as she handed me the almost empty bottle.

Johnson. Some name, huh? When she had said her name was Johnson, I didn't bother asking the origin. A woman like her wants to have a mysterious, tough edge. I know people, how to keep a situation moving smoothly, so I kept my curiosities to myself.

By this point I was pretty well plastered. I leaned past Johnson and watched the darkness swirl past the bus window. Johnson pulled me toward her and planted a soft, whiskey-flavored kiss on my lips.

"Are you trying to make yourself dizzy, looking out that window?" she whispered as she kept her mouth against mine. "You want dizzy? I'll make you dizzy."

Believe me, I certainly hadn't been dizzy for a while. Nancy had seen to that. She lost interest in sex about a month before this space thing happened. That's usually the way that time bomb ticked. First the sex and boom, the space.

"Yeah, make me dizzy, Johnson."

The name, Johnson, seemed weird as it slipped from my mouth. *Make me dizzy, Johnson?* Where the hell do these nose-pierced women get their names? Like Willi. Anyone who's peeked at her driver's license knows her real name is Laura Siegleman.

Now she goes by Willi. Just plain, no-last-name Willi. Seems pretty transient, if you ask me. Transient, like Johnson and I, traveling to Eugene in a dark bus.

Johnson kissed me again. The strong taste of whiskey aroused me. I ran my fingers through her hair. I kissed her eyes, her cheeks, her ears. Like high school lovers, we kissed over and over, wanting to go further, but taking our time. There was plenty of time, all the way to Eugene, maybe even Washington. I'd get my fingers in her pants and who knows when we'd stop. Maybe never.

Johnson raised her T-shirt. Substantial rectangular nipples bloomed like hard rosebuds on her small breasts. Even in the dark, I could see the glint of a gold hoop that pierced her overlarge nipple. The vision of that thin, gold wire penetrating her thick, chunky nipple was surprisingly erotic.

The nose ring I couldn't fathom, but the teeny wire in the nipple was hot, hot, hot. For some titillating reason the entire premise seemed to make perfect sense. I kissed my way down to the enticing decoration.

The delicate ring fit snugly on the tip of my tongue. I gently tugged the little hoop then flicked the nipple itself. First a light tug, then a quick flick while Johnson moaned quietly.

Yeah, it was about time I led a woman around by a ring. I plucked the golden circle then lapped the fleshy cube-like tip. I'd lead her around, like Nancy did to me, like Nancy's doing to Willi.

With three fast snaps, Johnson unbuttoned her jeans. Licking her nipple, pulling her by the hoop, I pushed my hand into her pants. Her pussy hair was

52

sparse, probably clipped into some wild punk design,
and her protruding lips were slippery. I wiggled my
fingers into her sliced flesh.

No . . . better yet . . . we'd be in line at the small
bus stop store. She'd be ahead of me buying her
smokes and I'd be one person back. The guy who
argued with himself all the way from Healdsburg
would be standing between us. In line, he'd start
debating about World War II.

Johnson turned to check him out. Apparently, her
seat toward the front of the bus that first couple
hundred miles hadn't afforded her the pleasure of
experiencing this guy. I, on the other hand, had sat
directly behind him. I knew by heart the sixteen
points favoring American intervention that he would
soon reiterate. The involuntary twitching of his
shoulder was the telltale signal that he was ready to
ramble.

Johnson looked past him to me. Her this-
guy's-a-nut look immediately shifted to a hey-
there's-another-dyke-on-the-bus nod. I returned her
acknowledgment with a smile.

Whenever two lesbians find themselves alone in a
group of straights, a magical camaraderie occurs.
Sooner or later, they cross the room and strike up a
conversation. It's a basic lesbian phenomenon —
strangers, ex-lovers, enemies. No matter how things
were yesterday, in a straight environment, we
gravitate.

If I had been in the right frame of mind that
enlightening day at the Rockfield Café, perhaps I
would have seen more than just Nancy and Willi.
Packed with straights, Willi and Nancy were drawn
together, from across a crowded heterosexual room.

It happens. Shit. Look at me and Johnson. One minute we're strangers, the next we're slugging whiskey in a bus stop rest room.

"No regrets?" I ran my finger across the bold letters on her T-shirt.

"Never." She belted the last swig of whiskey. "And you?" she challenged, her eyes shifting seductively.

"Not one," I lied. For in that very moment, I sincerely regretted that I wasn't already fucking her inside the bathroom stall. "Well, maybe one," I conceded.

"Yeah? And what's that?" She was teasing me big-time with her eyes.

She wanted me, no question about it. I pushed her into the stall and locked the door. Let Nancy have her good-for-nothing fling with Willi. Let Nancy have all the space she wanted. No skin off my teeth. Crammed in the stall, not needing space, Johnson and I were doing just fine.

Johnson started kissing me like she had suddenly ignited. Which she probably had, considering that without warning, the whiskey had unexpectedly hit me like a fast-flying freight train. I was reeling and Johnson was apparently switched on high.

She yanked her pants down and climbed on the toilet seat. Now eye level, her diagonally trimmed fur barely veiled her sassy thin lips like a collarless mink wrap. In contrast to the wildly bleached-blonde hairdo on her head, this hair was dark. Even so, with its flamboyant, angled style, it was just as reckless.

Bracing her hands over the top of the stall walls, Johnson raised her legs to my shoulders. The gorgeous sight this offered was unimaginable. Her

54

slender outer lips had parted and Johnson's blood-flushed sex was completely exposed.

Her clit seemed simple, unhampered by cumbersome folds. A wedge of narrow flesh seemed to point, like an arrow, toward its beaded ruby tip where the glans itself protruded slightly.

I had never seen a clit like hers. A slight split down the center of the berry-colored pearl resulted in two separate, but attached, pieces.

"Oh Jesus," I muttered as I fingered the double-humped miniature bulb.

"Double the pleasure." Johnson giggled as if she knew what I was referring to.

I pulled her lips with each index finger and ran my thumbs in small counter clockwise circles on each little orb.

Johnson started moaning and slippery cream seeped from her cunt. I dipped my thumbs in and spread it thickly over her jutting twin-heads. I rimmed her slit then twirled her clit and Johnson got crazy.

I wanted to do her in a different way — different than I had ever done anyone, different than anyone else had ever done her, and goddamnit, different than Willi was doing Nancy. I reached into my jacket pocket. There was nothing but a set of keys, some loose change, the cap from the whiskey and an emery board. Nothing . . . unless . . . I . . .

I pulled out the emery board. Used to be Nancy's, but not anymore, the rough-textured, coarse-and fine-sided nail file fit in my hand like another finger. Carefully, slowly, barely at all, I grazed the emery board against her nipple. I held her tit and rubbed the greedy nipple against the fine-grit side. With each consecutive scrape, Johnson got wilder. She pulled my hair, ripped at my shirt. So I gave her more — I switched to the coarse side, increased the friction till her nipple screamed fire-red.

Johnson's legs, still around my neck, pulled me in closer. Her pussy was back in my face. Her clit, seeping with sex drops, seemed to beg for what her rock-hard nipple was getting. I gave her what she wanted. I scraped the file against her clit shaft. Johnson let out a low growl. Oh yeah, I'd smooth down all the rough edges, baby. With more pressure, I pressed the file again. Oh baby oh!

Johnson squirmed. Glistening juice spurted from her red-rimmed opening. I jimmied the file to her pouting slit and traced the border with the sandpaper-like finger. Almost in, not quite, I wiggled against the pink portal. Back to the double beads, then again to the jellied entrance, I continued to churn her wide-open pussy.

Johnson started to jerk. I could imagine how the coarse side felt on her tender flesh. Lightly, carefully, I stimulated her. I'd bring her to the edge, I'd smooth her down, all right. My own cunt throbbed with aroused jealousy.

"Oh shit!" Johnson managed one long orgasmic cry.

No . . . better yet . . .

"I've been looking for you."

I pulled my gaze from the punk blonde as she climbed onto the bus. Nancy was standing right by my table.

"We need to talk," Nancy said, real apologetic-like.

I could get up, cross the street, jump on the bus and be on my way, just like that.

"We do?" I said coolly. I glanced back across the street. The bus doors had closed. From a window seat, Johnson seemed to be staring at me.

"I'm sorry, Claire," Nancy said as she rested her hand on my shoulder. "I've made a terrible mistake. You can't imagine the regrets I have."

"No regrets," I murmured, still staring at Johnson. The bus began to roll. If I ran, right now, across the street, I could flag down the bus. I could be sitting in the seat next to Johnson, one-two-three.

"What?" Nancy asked.

"Have a seat," I muttered. "There's plenty of space."

And with no regrets, I grabbed my jacket and raced toward the departing bus.

WINDOW SHOPPING

The good news about this town? On Saturday night at eleven o'clock, the adult bookstore is still open. The bad news is that it's the only place in town to buy a dildo. Call me sentimental, call me a creature of habit, but when Roxie moved out, she took the dildo. One month and two hours of masturbating later, I still couldn't get off.

Who would have thought I'd even have the need to do myself? Who would have thought I'd have this amount of time alone? Son of a bitch, masturbating at ten on a Saturday night and getting goddamn nowhere at all. Roxie got the dildo and I got the shaft.

Adult Books. The neon words shed an apocryphal red glow. Parked in my car, staring at the sign, I tried to muster the courage to go in. Even though the lot was nearly full and the place was probably hopping inside, the whole idea made me weak-kneed.

"I'd like to see your dildos," I said aloud, as if rehearsing would minimize my gnawing anxiety. I cleared my throat and tried again. "Your dildos, please?"

Nothing sounded right. I imagined the customers stopping in dead silence to watch me choose the thickest, largest dildo from the case.

"This one here?" I could hear the salesman say loudly as he pointed to the average-sized sex toy.

"No, the one right there." I'd gesture discreetly to the deluxe model, several dildos over.

"Oh, the Super Plunge!" His words would reverberate around the store as he pulled the dildo from the case and held it up for all to see.

The bookstore door swung open and an empty-handed man, hat low and trench coat tied shut, exited. He didn't look up once as he passed my car and headed toward a black sedan. I could understand why — eleven o'clock on a Saturday night. What did people do in there except shop? At least I had intention, at least I'd be carrying a bag when I came out of those doors.

A car pulled in. Another. Other people seemed to have no problem entering the bookstore. A black-laced, miniskirted woman swished past my car and disappeared into the building.

I'd count to fifty one last time and then, without

another thought, I'd get out of the car and walk right into the bookstore. No turning back. One, two, three, four, five . . .

A tall, heavy man appeared, no shopping bag in sight. Did people just window-shop in a place like that? Eighteen, nineteen, twenty, twenty-one . . . I'd simply go in, point to a dildo, trade some cash and get the hell out of there. No big deal.

What happened to the woman in black lace? Was she a hooker looking for some action? Thirty-five, thirty-six, thirty-seven, thirty-eight . . . Made sense, if she was. After all, people come to these establishments looking to buy easy sex. Like me, for fifty bucks, I'd have myself a new latex partner, no questions asked.

Forty-five, forty-six, forty-seven, forty-eight . . . I could go home. I could give Roxie a call and offer the bonsai for the dildo. I had a choice. Forty-nine, fifty. Shit.

Out in the cold and across the pavement, I headed toward the black door. The things I was willing to do for a long over-due orgasm. I'd go in, buy the dildo, then get out. This embarrassing ordeal would be over in seconds.

In contrast to the darkened parking lot, the bookstore was well lit. The thin, weasel-like guy behind the counter glanced up from an opened book with a slight nod. From a lingerie rack, a man peeked between the feather boas with a seedy smile. I felt suddenly nauseous. Where was everybody else?

"You okay?" The deep voice from behind startled me. "You looked kind of out of sorts when you came through the door."

A stocky woman moved in front of me. Her black

hair, clipped short around her face, tapered to a thin tail down her back. Although her eyes were cast with a disquieting hardness, a defiant playfulness flickered in their darkness. Thank God, a saleswoman.

"Maybe you could help me?" I said, almost whispering. The last person I wanted to know my business was the sleaze who lurked behind the lingerie.

"I'm certain I could." The woman moved closer, as if well aware of my concern. The high-style scent of her cologne brought images of exquisite emeralds, yet her rugged appearance — brown shirt tucked into faded jeans, work boots that had obviously seen better days — suggested no elegance. Seemingly unintentional, this offbeat contrast was curiously provocative.

"I need a dildo." I glanced to the lingerie rack then back to her.

"Any particular kind?" The woman's smile held a trace of amusement.

"Do you have a case or something?" Jesus. I should go directly to a phone booth and offer Roxie the bonsai *and* the roller blades. Hell, I'd even throw in the stereo.

"There are booths in the back." She pointed to a curtained doorway. "There's lots I could show you back there, nice and private."

"That's more like it," I said, relieved.

"Follow me." The woman grabbed my coat sleeve and led me past the drapes into a large hallway filled with doors.

"See, they got these films here — trust me, I know the right ones — and all you got to do is drop a few quarters in the slots." She opened a door and pulled me into a small booth. "Any kind of dildo you want to see, shit, any kind of anything you want to see, is right here on these little screens."

Standing behind me, she positioned me in front of a small television that was built into the wall. She dropped a bunch of quarters into the slot and quickly pushed the black button next to the TV. Differing sex scenarios flashed before me.

"Great dildo scene in this one," she said eagerly. She released the button.

Things had moved so swiftly that I barely had time to react. Crammed into an inconsiderable space, classy perfume swirling like a tiny hurricane, I stared, dumbfounded, at a video of three women sitting in a prison cell.

"It's about time you came around," the roughest of the women said sarcastically to the blonde femme dressed only in a tight undershirt and tiny white panties.

The T-shirt was so thin that I could see the woman's large areolas through the stretched material. Her nipples, distinct and hard, pushed against the taut shirt like raised arrows. Stirring excitement shot in all directions from between my legs. My clitoris throbbed, my nipples tightened.

"Maybe we should initiate her," the other butch woman said with a sexy sneer. "I mean, if she's so sincere and all."

"Anything," the blonde said softly. She pulled her shirt over her head.

The camera zeroed in for a side view of her breast. The nipple stood like a thick cranberry on a dark, round doily.

"Great tits," the woman behind me grunted.

I had to agree. So did the women in the prison cell.

"Great tits."

"Fuck yes."

The camera stayed fixed on the pouting nipple. Fingers grabbed the elongated cherry pit and tugged vigorously. The blonde moaned but the camera did not budge as it relentlessly recorded each hard pinch. The nipple tripled in size. The entire screen was red, erect flesh.

"So, you ready to join us, baby doll?"

The camera pulled back. The two butch women were circling the blonde. The blonde looked hot, like she was all ready to come, just from having her rosebuds squeezed.

"Yes, please," she begged.

A large-headed dildo, apparently carved from wood, was pulled from under the mattress of the upper bunk.

"Holy shit," I murmured. The memory of the super-dildo Roxie had confiscated suddenly shrank.

"Now *that's* a dildo." My newfound buddy's breath was hot in my ear.

One of the prisoners propped the blonde on a small table. The other lovingly caressed the wooden spear.

"Pull her panties aside."

Yeah, I thought, salivating. Pull them aside.

"You won't believe how she takes it," my cohort panted. She poured more quarters into the slot.

The camera zoomed to the crotch. The full vulva, housed behind the flimsy white cotton, burgeoned dramatically. The border of the panty crotch was quickly grasped but the hand refused to pull the aggravating veil aside.

Creamy wetness sopped my own panties as I watched. Barely able to breathe, I stared without blinking. My friend, whose erratic panting was loud and clear, wrapped her arms tight around me and pressed her belly against my ass.

"Okay, baby, here we go. Show us what you got for us."

"Yeah, sugar. Yeah, sugar. Show daddy what you got."

The panties were pulled aside revealing plump pink lips amidst a weaving of golden hair. Slowly, teasingly, the camera moved in. Wrinkled velvet flesh filled the screen.

"Oh, yes." The blonde rotated her cunt in small circles. *"I'm ready, Buzz."*

"C'mon, Buzz, give it to her."

As if drawing back honey-colored drapery, calloused fingers raised the large lips up and apart. The sex-drenched clitoris hung in full, glorious view. A clear gloss of moisture, shimmering like a slick coat of mineral oil on the blooming clit, settled in an oily puddle at the puckered point of entry.

"You already give yourself to Frankie?"

"No one!" the blonde said desperately. *"I've saved myself for you."*

In one swift thrust the finger entered the grinding slit, swirled in the pink cave and plucked back out. Pearl-colored dew smothered the fingertip. Two fingers pushed back in and twirled quickly.

"They're going to pop this cherry good," my

viewing partner muttered as more quarters clinked into the slot. "Real good. You wanted a dildo, here comes your dildo."

She pushed her hands under my shirt and squeezed my aching nipples. Pressed against my ass, she bucked against me, shoving me close to the screen. Her mouth was hot on my neck. She bit, she licked, she moaned.

On the screen, the bulb of the wooden dildo circled. The greasy entrance hungrily grasped at the smooth tip.

"Look at that ready snatch, Buzz. Ain't that a sight."

"Fuck me, please. Please!" The blonde attempted to push the bulbous dildo into her scarlet slit, to no avail.

My pants were being yanked to my knees. The slick scent of pussy filled the stuffy booth. From behind, I could feel my buddy struggling with her pants.

"You wanted a dildo? I'll give you a dildo." Her jeans unsnapped as she coaxed me with her words.

With strong hands, she separated my slippery thighs. I leaned against the wall, my face inches from the woman who now had the blonde's legs spread wide and was ready to plunge.

"Yeah, yeah," I mumbled. My mouth felt dry. My eyes burned. All the available moisture had accumulated in one splash-pool between my legs.

"God, you're wet!" As though the words came from deep in her throat, my companion's voice had lowered considerably.

I felt as if I had dropped an octave myself. My entire body seemed incredibly heavy. My legs trembled, my heart thumped in my chest.

"Shit if she ain't canned goods. Pop her hard, Buzz."

The camera zoomed back to the cherry-red opening. The flappy lips capped the dildo head like a fancy pink carnival hat.

"Push it in. Push it in," I whimpered. My eyes were glued to her gooey sex pocket as it slowly sucked in the wooden pleasure-giver.

"Like this, baby? You want it like this?"

A huge dildo rammed into my smoldering cunt. My entire vagina felt stretched beyond capacity. Filled completely, I groaned as merciless spasms surged through me.

"Ride me, sugar." My companion rocked her hips as she shoved the dildo in and out. In and out. In and out, she drove me.

As I took it hard, the blonde took it harder. The wood spearhead, covered with luminescent sap, snapped out of her slit then disappeared into the juicy pink. I wanted to drench my face in her golden pussy hair, soak my face in the abundant syrup, rub my face against her rubber-rigid clit lips.

"That's right, ride me good," my buddy mumbled.

I rotated my hips as she plunged deep. Her hand twisted in my hair, the other grasped my waist. The movie clicked off. The blonde was lost — I didn't care. The walls were closing in, the room was suddenly smaller. Sex vapor precipitated into little beads on the wall. Everything was slick, everything was wet.

Over and over, my booth-mate opened me hard.

Yanking my head back, jerking me onto the dildo, she went nonstop. Her legs were spread, she held her ground. With work boots, ritzy perfume and plenty of fire, she slammed me good.

I was close. I was ready to snap. There was no room to breathe. No place to fit. Tight tight tight tight tight tight tight.

I must have blacked out, because when I opened my eyes, I was alone, slouched in the corner of the booth. I stumbled into the corridor, through the curtained doorway and into the main room of the bookstore. The place was empty except for the weasel behind the counter.

"Need any help?" He barely looked up from his book.

"Nah," I shook my head and headed for the door. "Just window-shopping."

OPENING DOORS

Ellen Rose's life was as organized as her master suite closet. Arranged from short sleeve to long, then by color, her blouses were perfectly grouped. An assortment of designer pants filled the entire west wall of the closet. The shoes, neatly boxed and stacked by season, occupied the east wall shelves. From day dresses to expensive beaded gowns, every last item in her wardrobe had its place.

Because Ellen took the utmost pride in her sense of order, she was astonished to find herself locked out of the house. Had she been in that much of a hurry for her early-morning swim not to notice she had locked the door behind her?

In her sleek, wet bathing suit, Ellen hurried into the pool house. Winston normally kept a spare key taped behind the wall calendar, but the key was not there, nor was it in the abalone pencil holder that decorated the small wicker table. Irritated that she had inadvertently locked herself out, she sat on the edge of the faded-blue canvas chair and considered her options.

The chauffeur had left with her husband, Winston, for La Guardia. Ellen recalled the list of errands Winston had given the chauffeur and had no doubt he wouldn't be back before five. Maria and Lester both had the day off. The neighbors had a spare key but were cruising the Caribbean and wouldn't be home for three more days.

Frustrated, Ellen decided to search the small room again. Beneath the stack of last summer's magazines, under a half-read old paperback, back to the shell cup, but the key — which *should* have been behind the calendar — was missing.

"Damn Winston," she whispered under her breath. The poorly insulated pool house — hadn't she suggested they keep a portable heater available? — offered little warmth. Ellen's morning was undoubtedly off to a bad start.

She scanned the room, then noticed the phone lying on a pile of old phone books in the corner. "Well, at least Winston had had the sense to leave a phone here," she muttered to herself.

Ellen flipped through the Suffolk County yellow pages. Jammed with locksmiths, the listings seemed endless. This was Winston's job, for Christ's sake,

Ellen thought, annoyed. She handled the party lists, the household staff, the charities. Anything that involved hardware fell into Winston's realm.

Two days home from a week in Boston, on his way to Chicago, Winston had become less and less available over the last few months. Just as well, Ellen thought. When Winston was home, the entire house reverberated with an underlying tremor of disorder. Surely his last-minute, frantic search for his briefcase — Winston had stormed through the house in a rage, tossing things aside — contributed to her lockout. In a hurry to escape, she had raced to the pool, diving into deep blue oblivion an hour earlier than her usual schedule dictated.

Ellen's gaze drifted back to the yellow pages. "As if I know who to call," she mumbled. Could she even find a locksmith available at seven a.m.? If she had to, she'd offer cash plus bonus and as always, she'd have her way.

A large ad, boasting twenty-four-hour service, caught her eye. Perfect. Who needed Winston, after all?

"Anderson Locks, can I help you?"

"Yes, I need you to come right over."

"This is the answering service," the woman said curtly. Her voice sounded as if her nostrils had been pinched together with a clothespin. "I can get a message to the locksmith."

"The ad says twenty-four-hour service. I haven't

time to sit around while you pass messages back and forth. Connect me to the locksmith immediately." Ellen's words were clipped with a snobbish flair.

"Please hold."

Ellen heard a slight click. A picture of a gum-chewing woman, hands busy as she connected and disconnected phone lines, quickly came to mind. What did life offer to people who filled their hours with jobs such as that?

"Anderson here." The man's voice broke Ellen's thoughts.

"Yes, this is Mrs. Winston Rose, up at Rose Manor. I've locked myself out of the house. I'm dreadfully chilled. How soon can you be here?"

"Let's see, I've got a seven-thirty scheduled but I can send my daughter. She could leave right now, be there in . . . Rose Manor . . . your place is off Birch Terrace? Yeah, less then ten min —"

"Perhaps you don't understand, Mr. Anderson," Ellen interrupted. "This is Mrs. Rose, Mrs. *Winston* Rose. I'm locked out of my house and, *if I'm not mistaken,* this *is* a man's job. I have neither time nor patience to deal with an apprentice daughter tinkering with my locks. I've just come from a swim. I need immediate service."

"My girl's better than most in this town. Best I can do," he offered.

By the time she'd find another locksmith, Anderson's daughter could already have started the job. "Oh well, okay," Ellen conceded reluctantly. "Just get her here fast."

* * * * *

71

With a low groan, Chris veered the truck into the long driveway that led to the Rose estate. As far as she was concerned, her father's phone call had come one day too early. Last night, she had hung out at the club till closing, had one drink too many and could have used five more good hours of sleep.

"Shit," she complained to no one. "Day off, my ass."

She passed the thick grove of trees that lined the road and rounded a bend. A large Southern-style mansion came into view. Chris responded with a low whistle. No wonder dear old Dad insisted she do this job pronto.

Chris pulled up to the house and climbed out of the truck. Okay, she thought as she scoped the finely landscaped front, where's the damsel in distress?

At that moment, an elegant woman came from the side of the large home. Wrapped in an emerald green towel, her wet, auburn ringlets teasing her tan shoulders, she approached Chris.

"You the apprentice?" the woman snipped.

Her hotsy-totsy attitude immediately pulled Chris's don't-fuck-with-me trigger.

"You in a hurry, miss?" Chris said pointedly. Rich or no, Chris didn't take shit from anyone.

The color of the woman's eyes matched the green towel. Tiny freckles were splashed lightly across her sculptured nose. With damp hair and towel as her only accessories, she still had a wealthy, sophisticated look. Copper hair, painted pink toenails, long rich legs — this lady exuded royalty.

"Yes, I'm in a big hurry. Get my door open . . . that is, if *you* can."

Chris studied the sarcastic expression on the woman's face. Yeah, this lady was royalty all right. A royal bitch.

"Come around to the back. I couldn't bear you scratching the front terrace door with your tools."

Chris had an immediate urge to get back in her truck and haul ass. She didn't need this kind of crap, seven in the morning, on her day off. She weighed her temptation to split against her dad's probable reaction. No question, he'd raise hell if she pulled out now. *Scratch the terrace door with her tools.* Shit. Job or no, she was outta there. She had standards. She had self-respect. She didn't have to take shit from any high brow princess.

Mrs. Rose — with a walk that could get locks fixed for free — motioned for Chris to follow her toward the side of the house. Mesmerized by her round ass and sassy walk, Chris's staunch values quickly melted into a heated, syrupy feeling between her legs.

When it comes to business, sometimes one can't stand on ceremony, Chris rationalized silently. She studied Mrs. Rose's full ass swishing beneath the green towel. Hadn't her father insisted that the customer was always right?

They came around the side of the house to the back. Chris was impressed by the magnificence of the terraced gardens that covered the sloped section of the lawns. Red brick steps led from the back veranda, through the gardens, down to large, closely planted tall shrubs. Beyond that, to the right of the property was a rectangular-shaped pool and a small pool house.

"You know," Chris said, turning her attention back to Mrs. Rose, "breaking and entry is my specialty."

"Perhaps you should consider burglary then," Mrs. Rose said dryly.

"Yeah . . . maybe." Chris reached the back door. "Security system on?"

"Of course not." Mrs. Rose's tone had a cutting quality. "This was an accident."

Chris shot the woman a yeah-sure look then squatted to the lock. With a sly glance she appraised Mrs. Rose's slender calves, her half-hidden thighs. Tiny goose bumps covered the sun-tinted skin. God, would she like to break and enter Mrs. Strut-your-stuff-cold-as-ice Rose.

"I'm quite chilled." Mrs. Rose briskly ran her hands up and down her arms. "There's a nice bonus for you if you can get this done *tout de suite.*"

Chris cast a brief look at Mrs. Rose whose lips had taken on a slight bluish tint. "Put this on, you're freezing." Chris offered her jacket.

"Oh, I couldn't." She reached for the coat anyway.

The towel slipped to the ground and Chris was afforded a delicious view of Mrs. Rose in swimsuit alone. Wet, white and skintight, the suit hid nothing. Chris slowly caressed Mrs. Rose with her eyes. Her breasts swelled slightly to dark, hardened tips and her small waist flared to remarkably voluptuous hips. Beneath the stretched suit, a thick triangular thatch of hair feathered into tiny auburn strands which flirted from the suit's thigh border.

"Thanks." Mrs. Rose slipped into Chris's old alma mater jacket. The high school letters and sport's pins somewhat dissipated her otherwise hard edge. "I'll add a bonus for the use of the coat."

"Anytime something's done for you, you think you gotta pay?" Chris glanced at Mrs. Rose who, wrapped in the oversized jacket, looked suddenly vulnerable. Chris shook her head. "Damn. I'd hate to believe you gotta pay to be cared about."

Mrs. Rose shrugged silently and Chris noted a nonspecific sadness sheltered in her green eyes.

"I'm not charging for use of the jacket," Chris said as she fiddled with the lock. Fast — in expert time, really — the lock gave and the door clicked opened. She shifted up from her squat. "No charge for the lock either."

Why not give Mrs. Rose something to think about, Chris reasoned. She'd work the details out with Dad later.

"Oh please." Mrs. Rose hurried through the door, into the kitchen alcove and returned with a wad of cash. "Of course, I'll pay. Why, you've been so nice — your jacket, your attitude — and you've opened the lock so efficiently. How much do I owe you?"

Mrs. Rose's hair had begun to dry and small curls haphazardly framed her face. Seduced by the ringlets, the sprinkle of freckles, the hint of innocence in her eyes, Chris had a compelling urge to take her in her arms.

"How about a trade? Instead of cash, how about a quick dip in the pool?" Chris blurted. She pointed to the small swimming pin on the jacket. "Team champ. Damn. I haven't been in a pool since high school."

Mrs. Rose glanced toward the pool and then back to Chris. "Well, I suppose . . .

And why not a trade? Ellen considered the young woman standing before her. Short black hair, stocky build — the woman, attractive in a masculine sort of way, had an uncanny resemblance to her high school friend, Leslie Simpson. Leslie "Best Friends Forever" Simpson. Who cared about cheerleading when she had Leslie? Who cared about parties or dresses or even boys? They were best friends, closer than anyone, until Ellen's parents had broken up their friendship and sent her to boarding school.

What harm was there in a simple dip in the pool? After all, she hadn't had a swimming companion since . . . Why, she hadn't had a *real* friend since she married Winston. He had introduced her to society's finest, insisting that she abandon her old friends. *Past history, past tense* — that was Winston's view of Ellen's life prior to his grand entrance. Since then, enmeshed in parties and society balls, surrounded by people, Ellen realized she'd been haunted by a vacant loneliness.

"C'mon," the locksmith challenged. "I'll race you." She tossed her tools on the porch step and headed toward the pool.

"A suit —?" Ellen called after her, but the woman was already halfway to the pool, stripping off her shirt as she ran.

In a white sleeveless T-shirt and striped boxer shorts, the locksmith dove into the deep end. Ellen slowly stepped down the red brick steps.

"Whoa, it'll wake you up all right!" the locksmith shouted from the water.

Ellen unsnapped the jacket, remembering Leslie — holding hands with Leslie, giggling with Leslie, slow dancing with Leslie, skinny dipping at the water hole with Leslie. Leslie. Leslie. Leslie.

Ellen pulled off her white stretch suit and dove into the cold.

From underwater, with eyes open, Chris saw her. Like a beautiful mermaid, Mrs. Rose moved gracefully toward her. Her breasts boasted tiny hardened nipples that matched the rosy pink of her lips. A small protrusion of flesh jutted from the auburn-covered pussy lips, the same color as her nipples. Desperate to stay below, Chris reluctantly headed for air. Within seconds, Mrs. Rose surfaced, right at her side.

"Being naked in the water reminds me of the old days when I felt so free." Mrs. Rose smiled. She let her feet reach the floor of the pool. The water barely covered her shoulders.

Chris concentrated on her blush-rose lips but could only think of the berry nipples and pulpy pink clit hidden beneath the water. "And you look so beautiful, free."

"Really? Do you *really* think so?" Mrs. Rose's voice sounded like a young girl.

Chris wanted to reach for her, to touch her lips, to take her in her arms and press against her. Uncertain, she didn't move. "Yes, I really think so."

"I had a friend once," Mrs. Rose almost

whispered. "A lot like you. Best friends, forever. But she's gone now. I've no friends anymore. Not really."

"I'll be your friend," Chris murmured. "I'll be anything you want." Oh shit, Chris thought. She was diving off an internal deep end. Best friends with Mrs. Winston Rose. Yeah, right.

"Really?" Mrs. Rose moved even closer. "We used to hold hands and slow dance. If you were my friend, would you hold my hand and slow dance, too?"

Chris took Mrs. Rose in her arms. From the wet silkiness of her delicate body, the coolness of her naked skin, an enchanting melody seemed to radiate. Holding Mrs. Rose, Chris swayed to the music.

"Like this? Is this how you danced?" Chris said softly.

Yes.

Had Mrs. Rose answered? The trees, the blooming flowers, the sun pushing through the morning gray — the whole world seemed to be whispering. *Yes, this is just what I want.*

Chris kissed Mrs. Rose's sugar-sweet mouth. Her luscious lips, her smooth cheeks, her exquisite neck — Chris showered her in tiny kisses as they swayed in the water, arm in arm.

"It's been so long since anyone has really cared about me," Mrs. Rose confessed. "So long."

Consumed by overwhelming desire, Chris struggled with the urge to scoop Mrs. Rose into her arms and carry her to the edge of the pool. She fantasized propping Mrs. Rose's legs on the Italian-tiled ledge as she cradled her upper torso in the water. Water, bubbling from the jet, would tumble against Mrs. Rose's clitoris. And Chris would kiss her, over and over, would whisper how hot, how beautiful, how exciting she was. She'd pinch her hardened nipples. She'd nip her tightened areolas. She'd pull the skin above her auburn thatch of hair and expose the satin-red flesh.

That vision of Mrs. Rose was difficult to erase. Chris imagined slicing her fingers into Mrs. Rose's secret folds and slowly sliding back and forth across the generous clit. She'd stir her fingers into the oily moisture — thicker than water, more slippery than water — in search of her opening. The water would quickly beat against Mrs. Rose's cunt — push, prod, flatten against Mrs. Rose's cunt.

Into the gaping slit, Chris would bury her finger. She'd jiggle it in fast, tapping strokes. Her fingertip would dance hard on the rough-textured G spot. Chris knew how to bring a woman to her pleasure. She'd hold her strong. She'd guide Mrs. Rose's throbbing clitoris closer and closer toward the pounding stream of water and wouldn't back off. Mrs. Rose would squirm and moan. She'd resist at first, but finally give in.

Chris envisioned Mrs. Rose arched in all-consuming passion. She'd set her free all right. She'd set her absolutely, once and for all, free. Slow dancing in the water, Mrs. Rose quiet in her arms, Chris hesitated momentarily then made her move. With one fast motion, she lifted Mrs. Rose into her arms and headed toward the pool's edge.

In the locksmith's arms, everything else seemed to disappear. Ellen had no idea why she felt so safe, but chose not to question. Through the water, to the edge of the pool, the woman carried Ellen.

"Where can we go?" the locksmith's words flowed slowly, like the water lapping the sides of the pool.

Ellen hesitated, suddenly overwhelmed with how much of the estate was saturated with Winston. The only place she felt was hers was her bedroom. There, her colors, her scents, her dreams and desires were stockpiled.

"My room," Ellen finally said and motioned toward the house.

At the red brick stairs, the locksmith grabbed her jacket and wrapped it around Ellen. They crossed the veranda and went into the kitchen. With shy words, Ellen guided the woman through the marbled entranceway, up the circular staircase, down the long hallway, to the master suite.

As they came into her room, Ellen's first thoughts — that her bed wasn't made and the closet door was swung wide open — filled her with anxiety. In the race to escape Winston's tirade, she had left her life in disarray. "Under normal circumstances," Ellen whispered before the locksmith could judge, "things would be in proper order. It's just that I —" But a passionate kiss interrupted her words.

Chris stepped out of her boxers, pulled off her T-shirt and together, she and Mrs. Rose sank into the bed. The sheets were mint green clouds and the comforter was a feather dream. More kisses and then more. Mrs. Rose's lips were like satin rose petals. Thirsty for their sweetness, Chris drew them into her mouth and gently suckled.

Mrs. Rose was lovely and open and soft. The swell of her breasts, the indentation of her waist, the fullness of her hips — she was a luscious beauty. Chris caressed her lightly, as if Mrs. Rose were a porcelain treasure, easily broken by a heavy hand.

As if being called to do so, Chris looked into Mrs. Rose's eyes. Riding a single tear, a story of sad words balanced on the fringe of Mrs. Rose's auburn lashes.

"Are you okay?" Chris partially sat up. She rescued the small tear with her fingertip. "I don't want to make you sad."

"I want you to care, that's all." Mrs. Rose glanced away.

A rushing sensation filled Chris's heart. "What's your name?"

"Ellen."

Their eyes met again.

"Ellen Rose." Chris let the name roll across her tongue. "I'm Chris."

"Chris — the locksmith's daughter," Ellen said with an apologetic smile. "I'm sorry I was so —"

The heated kiss that silenced Ellen quickly melted her iceberg thoughts. The disgraceful way she had talked to Chris became a vague gray. The unpalatable fact that her bed was unmade and messy, wavered, then dissolved. And the image of her closet door, seemingly flung open with unpardonable carelessness, vanished.

Yes, the kiss that silenced Ellen swiftly carried her from an bleak environment of order to a jumbled world of colors. She swirled in light blues as Chris's kisses moved from her neck to the curve of her breasts. Yellows and greens enveloped her as Chris slipped Ellen's hardened nipple into her mouth. Orange lifted and twirled her as Chris licked her belly. Chris's tongue fluttered against Ellen's secret flesh and bright reds filled the room. Brilliant purples and blues crashed through the windows, the door, the walls.

Chris flicked Ellen's aching clitoris. She slowly inched her fingers in, then out, in then out of Ellen's pulsating opening. Ellen arched up. She dug her nails into Chris's back On and on, over and over, Chris penetrated deep into her. Chris kneaded and rubbed, thrust and massaged until a prism of colors, a kaleidoscope of colors, a panorama of colors spilled into the room and splashed across the walls.

When Ellen finally climbed out of bed, it was after one. Wrapped in a sheet and nothing more, she went directly to her closet. She reached for a swimsuit and turned to leave, but hesitated. Suddenly provoked, but uncertain why, she intermingled several short-sleeved shirts into the pants section. An immediate urge to set things back in order rushed through her, but instead, she pushed herself on, mixing the day dresses with the beaded gowns and scattering shoes onto the closet floor.

In the midday heat, Ellen sat by the pool. The sun soothed her. Only a few times did she consider the disorganized clothing, the messed bed, and the flung-open closet door — the rest of the day, she tanned.

AIM TO PLEASE

An unwilling victim to her wild and kinky tendencies, my Gina, I could tell, was intrigued by last night's events. Although Gina professed that her butch buddy, Terry, had put her reputation on the line by exiting the bar, arm in arm, with some motorcycle butch, Gina's lapis blue eyes glittered as she spoke and a subtle excitement lined each word.

"Shit," Gina smirked, shaking her head. "Stone butch on stone butch, can you imagine those two trying to fuck?"

Actually, I *could* imagine the scenario vividly, but I didn't say a word.

"Put two butches together and soon enough you'll find out which one ain't really butch," Gina snickered, although her spill-the-beans eyes said otherwise.

"Not necessarily," I said nonchalantly. I fiddled with the lace on my pillowcase. "Some butches, on occasion, like to experiment. No big deal."

"*No big deal?*" Gina climbed out of bed and headed toward the bathroom. Her muscles were flexed and her walk, exaggerated. She stopped in front of the mirror and gestured with attitude. "You'd never catch me with another butch. For what? A good laugh? As if topping me were possible —" Puffed like a colorful bird parading her plumage, she offhandedly posed in front of the mirror. "Shit, what the hell was Terry thinking?"

It didn't matter what she said or how much she flexed in front of that mirror. There was absolutely no doubt in my mind — the concept of being topped by a butch titillated Gina. A stud-hot butch who almost swaggered from the weight of her I'm-on-top pride, Gina was attempting to mask her forbidden desires. But I could see down to her make-me-a-bottom core. Hard as she tried, Gina has no secrets — never had, never will — not from me. Her taboo, private passions were obvious. After all, I'm her femme.

That's how it all began — Sunday morning, in bed with Gina, listening to her snide remarks about Terry. I didn't press the issue. Instead, as Gina rambled on about the outrageousness of a butch topping a butch, I silently schemed. I planned on giving my Gina just what she wanted.

My ex-lover, Marty, was Ms. Leather two years straight. She's tough, she's butch and she's very, very top. Living three hours away, in the middle of nowhere, she'd drive anywhere for the right adventure. I knew this about Marty. I knew Marty inside out.

"So are you up for a little game?" I said to Gina, over dinner on Monday.

"Cards?" Gina said, distracted by the football game on TV.

"No, sweetie." I hesitated momentarily and then added seductively, "I mean a *game* game."

My tone must have bull's-eyed because Gina immediately turned to me. A hot smile crossed her face. "Oh, yeah? And what does my baby have in mind?"

"Maybe I could blindfold *you* this time?" I thought back to the last game we played. Gina had blindfolded me with a silk scarf, tied me to the bed and taken complete control.

"And then what?" Gina looked straight at me.

"And then . . ." I let the words trail into a whisper. ". . . I'd take over."

"And . . . ?"

"And anything goes," I murmured, pausing for added effect. "Anything."

I noted the tiny sparkle in Gina's eyes. The hint of a smile flirted with her full-lipped mouth and I immediately thought of her pussy. I imagined dressing her in white lace panties and watching as Marty pulled the crotch aside to expose her blonde-furred lips.

Marty would take over. Marty would do all the things I dreamed of doing but wasn't capable of — like strapping on a dildo and wrapping Gina around my waist. Marty was, strong, Marty could bounce Gina up and down and slam into her simultaneously. Marty, all bis and tris and power plunge could pound her fingers into Gina nonstop. I lose momentum, I fall short. Marty could lift her, could twirl her like a baton. Marty, strong as steel, could go on and on.

Marty was hot, hot, hot. On several occasions she had called and asked to see me on the side. Gina and I played our games, but we had a strict agreement: no extracurricular sex adventures. As much as I fantasized about a discreet night or two alone with Marty, I never acted on it. After all, I love Gina. I'd do anything for Gina.

"Anything goes, huh?" Gina laughed.

I nodded provocatively.

"You're on."

"Friday night." My voice simmered with a femme-top edge.

"Friday night," she agreed.

I rented a motel room and stocked it in advance. Whiskey for Marty — Marty loves Jack Daniels —

and bourbon for Gina. I made a cassette especially for the occasion. Marty likes the sounds of a smoked-filled café so I included plenty of sultry saxophone.

Restraints for Gina's hands and legs, dildo, harness, lube — I had everything in place. Room 159. Gina would be tied to the bed and blindfolded when Marty came through the unlocked door at ten.

Bourbon at the bar, a quiet dinner for two . . . the evening couldn't have gone any smoother. Although I had insisted our game not be discussed, the image of Marty taking Gina dominated my thoughts. I had difficulty concentrating on the conversation. Gina appeared just as consumed as I was. Anticipation and excitement swirled in her eyes. She sparked, she glowed. Passion sizzled in her words. As I watched Gina, I visualized Marty in her black and gold Mercedes, heading toward town. Nine-fifteen. I dipped my finger in Gina's chocolate mousse and teased the cool dessert along her playful tongue.

Gina covered her finger in a thick layer of mousse and offered it to me. I shook my head.

"No dessert?" she asked, surprised.

Without a word, I smiled. I'd have my dessert soon enough.

I pulled into the motel lot. Nine-forty-five. Gina was next to me, blindfold intact. "You ready, Baby?" I teased. *Baby* was her pet name for me but from this moment on, the tables were turned. Tonight Gina was my baby. Tonight Gina would be Marty's baby, too.

To the room, I led her. To the bed, to the ties
awaiting her, I took her all the way. I clicked the
music on high, slowly removed her clothes and tied
her spread-eagle, face down. I poured her a bourbon
but drank it myself. My reflection in the mirror
gazed back at me seductively.

*Any moment now, Marty will come through that
door . . .*

I painted more lipstick on my lips.

. . . any moment, I'll hand her a Jack Daniels.

I licked my lips, making them shiny wet. I
looked sexy, I looked delicious, I looked femme-wild.

"You're teasing me, Darla. What's the wait?"
Blindfolded, Gina squirmed on the bed.

"Just looking at your fine ass, baby. Just making
you crazy for me." Suddenly nervous, I refilled the
glass and gulped it down. Seconds later, the door
opened and Marty — black boots and silver-tips,
leather vest and no shirt, tight jeans ripped at the
thighs — stepped in the room. Everything was
spinning, except for Marty who stood firm in the
cyclone's center.

"Hello, doll." She mouthed the words without
making a sound. She shot me her cocksure grin and
licked her lips.

Hell of a long time since I'd been called doll. *Let
me have you, doll. You know I'm crazy for you, doll.
Spread your legs for me, doll. Doll. Doll. Doll.* My
heart began to pound. As if riding her
cut-to-the-chase cologne, Marty's presence permeated
the room.

"Nice perfume, baby. You went all out for
tonight, didn't you," Gina murmured, obviously
unaware of Marty's presence.

Gina seemed far away and I made no effort to reply. Instead, unable to turn away, I stared at Marty.

"I missed you, doll," Marty said intently, although, hidden behind the music, her words were barely audible.

Hot cream seeped through my body and churned in my pussy.

"C'mon, baby," Gina moaned from the bed.

I pointed to Gina but Marty pointed to me. Again, I pointed to Gina. Marty's smile broke into a silent laugh. She shook her head and pointed, once again, to me. Did she want me to top Gina? I was certain I had made it clear — she would top Gina, I would watch.

Marty stepped toward me. I didn't budge. Another step, close to me, next to me, she pushed me onto the table and kissed me hard. The bottle of Jack Daniels fell to the carpet with a clunk.

Secured to the bed, Gina tried to turn to her side, to no avail. "Whatcha doing, baby?"

"Taking my time," I muttered between Marty's desperate kisses. She ripped my shirt opened and roughly grabbed my breasts. I moaned with pleasure.

"Tell her you're masturbating. Tell her to lift her ass, show you what she's got," Marty demanded in my ear.

"I'm touching myself and watching you," I said faintly. "Lift your ass. Show me what you've got."

"Oh, God," Gina pleaded. "Take off my blindfold. Let me watch you."

Marty pushed her hand up my skirt, pulled my panties aside and slammed into my wetness. All bis, tris and power plunge, she went nonstop. I glanced at Gina, ass up and vulnerable, and imagined Marty fucking her. She'd strap on the dildo, she'd give it to her nice and hard.

Marty plunged into me, three fingers, four fingers. *Oh yes, baby. Oh yes, baby* — I wanted to moan, I wanted to scream, I wanted to cry out Marty's name. Biting my lip, I held in my pleasure.

The table rocked as she drove into me. Marty didn't care, one wild sweep of her arm and the table cleared completely. My drink spilled, the lube and dildo tumbled to the floor. Earthquake starter, thunderstorm maker — the room whirled with Marty's torrential energy.

"That's it, doll. That's it." Marty's fiery words hissed in my ear. Her breath, ignited with quick, shallow pants, launched surging heat waves. I dug my nails into her back. I bit her shoulder, leaving dark red marks. Rock-hard, sweet Marty didn't flinch.

"Baby, whatcha doing?" Hurricane winds muffled Gina's words.

"Watching you," I gasped.

Marty lifted me from the table and pressed me against the wall. She tore open my blouse and tugged down my bra. Burning kisses seared my neck, my shoulder, the curve of my breast. Blood-flushed and thick, my nipples flared with desire.

"Is this what you want, doll?" Marty whispered.

She sucked the fever-pink tip of my breast into her mouth. An involuntary cry slipped from my lips.

"Who's with you?" Gina's voice's cut through the

windstorm, cut through the thunder, cut through the sudden silence. I glanced at the cassette player — side one had finished playing.

Abruptly, Marty loosened her tight grip. Unpredictable as hell, she tossed me a dangerous smile and then, as though an afterthought, headed toward Gina.

"You got a problem, butch girl?" She untied Gina's legs.

"Who wants to know?" Gina said, with smart-ass attitude.

That's my Gina. Damn, if she couldn't blend into any situation. Gina liked a good time, all right.

Marty untied Gina's blindfold, grabbed a handful of hair and jerked Gina's face from the pillows.

"Inquiring minds want to know, right Darla?" Marty gestured to me.

"You *did* say anything goes," I reminded Gina, just in case her butch bravado was getting ready to enter the scene.

"I suppose I did," she conceded like a helpless victim of circumstances. But I knew Gina, I could read it in her eyes, she wanted whatever Marty had to offer. After a quick butch game of It's Out Of My Control we could get on with things.

"It's out of your control, then, isn't it," I said smugly.

Gina was quiet but her eyes sparkled. "I guess so . . ."

"You guessed right," Marty interjected. She flipped the tape, clicked on the music and grabbed the Jack Daniels. Downing her share in a fast gulp, she offered the bottle to Gina.

"Bourbon's *my* drink." Gina glanced at me with a butch tell-me-you-didn't-bring-bourbon look.

With an of-course-I-did femme smile, I surveyed the floor for the bottle of bourbon. Marty grabbed the dildo and harness in one hand and the bourbon in the other.

"Like it straight up?" she asked untying Gina's wrists and handing her the bottle. "Or don't you know?"

No answer. Sitting on the edge of the bed, Gina belted down the bourbon as Marty pushed the dildo through the harness and strapped it around her hips. With a fistful of lube, she greased the thick, lavender toy directly in front of Gina who gulped bourbon with each long stroke Marty made.

Filled with throbbing anticipation, I leaned against the wall. I'd seen Marty don a strap-on many times before and knew, all too well, what to expect. Marty winked at me, like she used to, seconds before she'd lift me in the air and sink me onto her belted-on tool. God, she was hot as hell when she gave me that look. Hot as fucking hell.

In one fast move, she lifted Gina. With a long, low cry, Gina wrapped her arms around Marty's shoulders and her legs around Marty's waist and the dildo disappeared between my two women.

Marty grabbed Gina's ass and bounced her up and down — the dildo a delicious focal point. In the corner, against the wall, I slid to the floor. Gina was wet, I could smell her scent. I could hear the slapping sound of each penetrating thrust.

I thought of her pussy — her puffy, blonde pussy — sucking in that hard spear. Marty rocked it.

Marty rolled it. Marty drove it home. My pussy was juiced-up. My pussy was soaking. I twirled my fingers against my clit in fast figure-eights. *That's it, Gina. Take it all, Gina.*

With demanding urgency, Gina's moans reached a crescendo. She was on the edge, she was ready to pop. I crawled across the room and positioned myself at Marty's feet, directly beneath Gina's full ass. The purple intruder, milky-wet, pierced Gina's hungry slit.

Up Marty raised her, down Marty slammed her while I pushed and pulled Gina's ass. Marty got wilder, Gina crazier. I burrowed my finger between Gina's checks and teased the swollen entrance of her ass.

Without warning, Marty stepped around me, Gina in tow. Bobbing Gina on the dildo, she crossed the room and disappeared into the bathroom. They rammed against the wall, smashed against the bathroom door.

Gina's cries of pleasure were muffled by Marty's insistent voice. "Like it now, baby? Huh, baby? I'll fuck you, yeah, I'll fuck you good."

The door thumped without letup. Gina moaned repeatedly. Ready to burst with desire, I hurried to join the party progress. I jiggled the knob but the locked door wouldn't open.

"Hey, open up."

The noise in the bathroom came to a sudden stop.

"C'mon, let me in."

I heard whispering and low laughs, but no other response.

"Can't I play, too?" My voice shifted into ultimate femme fatale.

Momentary silence, then the lock clicked.

"Can you play, too?" Marty said, partially opening the door. Beads of sweat teased her upper lip. "What do ya say, Gina? Can Darla play?"

From behind Marty, with her face flushed and hair damp, Gina nodded. "I don't see why not. After all, she's been such a sweet girl — always aiming to please her woman."

Marty, all bis and tris, stepped from the bathroom with Gina right behind. Saturated with the fragrance of sex, they surrounded me, both of them kissing me relentlessly. My blouse was pulled off and my skirt fell to the ground. With one sharp snap, my panties were ripped off and tied around my eyes. Blindfolded, I was lifted, carried, pushed against the wall. Thick fingers pushed into my throbbing cunt. Fast hands squeezed my desire-thickened nipples.

"Go ahead, give it to her." Gina's voice was gruff as she pulled my back against her naked body. Using her arms as a body harness, she propped me in the air. My legs were separated as Marty pressed her way in.

"Yeah, yeah doll," Marty panted.

The dildo slowly pressed at my entrance. With a fast, impatient jerk, Gina lunged forward and the dildo, suddenly feeling larger than it had looked, sank deep into me. Gina and Marty moved simultaneously. Forward, then back, forward then back, as if engaged in a frenzied two-step, they maintained an ongoing, jarring rhythm.

Again and again, Marty, her legs like steel

girders, her hips nonstop, thundered into me. Her sweat, sweetened with beads of cologne, drizzled like a tiny rain shower across my face and breasts. I was swept in the wild winds, whirling in the electrical storm of Marty's repeated thrusts.

Gina — strong as ever, tough as ever — held me firm. She sat me on the dildo, twisted on the dildo, pushed me down, dragged me up, made me crazy.

"So close, so close," I cried.

And both women, knowing my pleasures so well, suddenly stopped. Grip tight, Gina kept me propped as Marty quickly, yet precisely, twitched the tip of the dildo on my G spot. An expert, Marty continued to jerk in rapid, short strokes.

Gina dug her nails into me and pierced my shoulder with sharp bites. On and on and on they went, moving yet still, fast yet achingly slow, until finally, with long-awaited agony, I surrendered into sense-crashing release.

Saturday morning, when I awoke, Gina was stroking my hair. "My sweet baby," she whispered.

I closed my eyes with complete satisfaction. There was nothing like pleasing your woman.

HOT SUMMER NIGHT

It was a breezeless night, a toss and turn, kick-the-sheets-off night. Betsey was restless, couldn't sleep. She lay awake, staring into blackness. The ceiling fan's monotonous drone lulled Betsey into indiscriminate reprieves and sporadically, her edginess would dissipate. As though free-falling in night-cloaked daydreams, Betsey slid in and out of disjointed fantasies.

"I love you forever, Jewells," Betsey whispered to a fleeting mirage whose shimmering fingers teased the swell of her breast, the indentation of her waist, the curve of her full hips, with summer-heat caresses.

A light tinkling of wind chimes chased the vision. Betsey listened intently to the gentle, thin song and contemplated the stirring of a faint breeze. A lonely night, a sultry night, with nothing but the wind chimes to murmur in her ear.

"Damn you, Jewells!" Betsey kicked away the twisted sheets tangled at her feet and climbed out of bed. The hardwood floor seduced her feet with unexpected coolness. In the dark, Betsey stood, thinking of contradictions, thinking of Jewells.

During the year with Jewells, time had raced like thunderbolt thoroughbreds. Lover, best friend, confidant, partner — Jewells had invaded Betsey's heart, claiming overwhelming victory. Betsey had surrendered without a struggle. Twelve fleeting months ... how drawn out they seemed in retrospect. Each memory passed, agonizingly slowly. Every touch, every whisper was magnetized and expanded.

In the middle of her room, captured by melodious memories, Betsey swayed to the sweetly clinking wind chimes. Lost in a dreamy waltz, she danced with the fantasy of Jewells. She was filled with an insatiable craving for the way things had been.

The roar of an approaching car cut into the night, shattering the spell. Betsey's pulse quickened, relentlessly pounding. After midnight, burning the quiet streets, rustling up dormant hopes — it had to be Jewells.

Betsey, her wispy silk gown clinging, hurried through the house to the front porch. Haloed by the light of the moon, she waited for the oncoming car to round the bend. A gentle wind whispered, coaxing the flimsy nightie between Betsey's thighs. Her nipples stood hard, although the air was warm.

Anticipation aroused her. Any second, the headlights would announce Jewells's arrival. Any second, Betsey would run barefoot to the street. Any second, any second . . .

The car lights ricocheted from house to house, to trees lining the road, to the street itself. *Here she comes.* A rush of butterflies scattered in Betsey's heart and she broke into a sprint.

Jewells, here I am. On the sidewalk's edge, she danced in white silk as Jewells's convertible drew to a fast stop. Bandanna around her straight, blonde hair, a diamond hoop in her ear, Jewells just smiled. Her smile, that telltale smile, said all the words.

"It was so hot, I was restless —" Betsey's own words sounded muffled as tidal waves of exhilaration crashed through her.

"I know." Jewells leaned, opening the passenger door.

Had heat lightning flashed in the sky? Betsey was uncertain. She climbed into the car, surrounded by electrical storms, and silently peered straight ahead. Tonight there was nothing but what lay ahead. Jewells gunned the motor and the car thundered. Top down, a sticky night, they sped off in search of relief.

They soared out of town onto barren country roads where the heat suddenly splintered into refreshing cool air. Distant trees, with branches hidden beneath knitted leaves, dotted the fields. Where they were headed, Betsey didn't care, not with the cool air whipping through her hair, not when Jewells was leading the way.

Jewells had been out of Betsey's life for a few short months. It seemed like years, an eternity. But it was Betsey's choice. It had been a hard decision. Having loved Jewells beyond reason, Betsey had tried everything to live in the shadowy world that Jewells had created. Jewells had said they'd be together forever, meant forever, and every few weeks, after midnight, she'd zoom by Betsey's house and tempt fate. Perhaps to remind Betsey that she was still waiting, perhaps to raise the ante — whatever the reason, it didn't matter. Betsey would lie in bed and, with the stakes so high, fight the urge to take one more card.

"I've missed you — you know I have." Jewells's words battled the rushing wind.

Betsey nodded, but did not turn her gaze from the oncoming dark road — not that second nor the next, when Jewells's hand drifted to her silk-draped thigh. A simple touch launched hundreds of swirling memories. Piercing pleasure leapt from Jewells's fingertips, surged through Betsey's body, and penetrated deep between her legs. Betsey suppressed an involuntary moan.

"Haven't you missed me? My touch?" Jewells slipped her hand beneath the nightie.

Bathed in the moon's glow, Betsey's gown poured smoothly over her soft curves like heavy whipping cream. Vivid visions from the past — Jewells streaking thick cream across Betsey's mouth, to her hardened nipples and down to her secret hair — spun in her mind like a sparkling crystal. Not unlike tonight, that night had also been sultry and humid. Jewells and Betsey had lain in bed watching the ceiling fan whirl. Talking about breaking the heat, they ended up naked on the kitchen floor, squeezed together in front of the opened refrigerator.

"Second only to being fanned by palm leaves," Jewells had said with a cool smile. She dipped her finger in softly beaten, sugared cream and traced the sweetness across Betsey's lips. Then, with one of her knee-knocking kisses, Jewells sucked the tempting dessert into her own mouth.

Still kissing Betsey, Jewells managed to steal another scoop. Slowly she spread the whiteness across Betsey's breasts and down her round belly.

"I'll paint a satin gown on you and undress you with kisses," Jewells said as she smothered her with hungry kisses.

With Jewells, reality melted into shimmering fantasies. Effortlessly, delicious cream transformed to a Cinderella gown; cherry jello glittered, expensive rubies. On the kitchen floor — or was it indeed, as Jewells said, a royal boudoir? — Betsey swirled in exotic sensations.

Betsey's nipples poked from the whipping cream like thick, red rocks. Her clitoris ached with excitement. Jewells, with a look that could thaw ice blocks, slathered the jello up and down Betsey's thighs, then, spreading her legs, lapped the sweet concoction with loud slurps.

"Princess," she muttered between cherry kisses. In fast circles, she smeared the whipping cream, warming Betsey's belly with her strokes.

Betsey — eyes closed tight — could feel a diamond tiara in her hair, a regal gown flowing across her body. She was Jewells's princess. She was beautiful and splendid and anything else Jewells told her to be.

Jewells dipped the jello into Betsey's desire-opened sex. The cold gelatin slid into the folds and quickly warmed. Twirling the jello on her fingers, Jewells pushed slightly into the tight slit.

"I'll fuck you sweet..." Jewells hesitated momentarily and then thrust deep. "...Princess."

She alternated between forcing jello into Betsey's vagina and sucking it back out. One hand scooped the jello while the other pressed the mons back, exposing Betsey's clit which now happily collided with Jewells's nose.

Betsey ran her fingers across her nipples and licked the warmed cream from her fingertips — back and forth, back and forth — as Jewells whipped her into ecstasy.

As the car raced into the moonlight, Betsey ran her fingers across her nightie and brought them to her mouth. She could almost taste whipping cream. That's how it was with Jewells, fantasy coiled into fantasy. Which was nice, so very nice, so incredibly, wonderfully, nice... except for the discomforting fact that there was no real reality with Jewells. Never.

All too late, Betsey had found that her relationship with Jewells was a hall of mirrors. Jewells could shadow dance, could outshine, could be anything Betsey wanted her to be, except honest.

Lies. Lies. Lies. Betsey glanced at Jewells, who stared out past the road into the darkness. Her diamond earring glittered in the moonlight as if promising a better tomorrow. The pot was sweet but the stakes were high. Too high.

I should tell her to take me home. I should make her turn around this very instant. The words flickered lightly in Betsey's mind and then exploded into a vivid picture of that day at the beach, last summer, with Jewells. *Turn around this very instant.*

"Turn around," Jewells had called to Betsey as she walked toward the ocean.

Betsey had kept walking, a smile on her face.

"Turn around this very instant!" Jewells's yell was muffled by the ocean's surf.

In a hidden alcove, they had picnicked. Jewells had filled baskets with freshly baked bread, an array of cheese and fruit, wine and flowers — lots of flowers, a basket filled only with flowers. On a checkered cloth, they lay lazily in the hot sun until Betsey, without a word, headed for the water.

Although the sun was hot, the ocean breeze was cool. Betsey, dressed in shorts and a halter top, stood in the wet sand and stared out to the horizon.

"Turn around for me, Betsey." This time the voice was softer, closer, right in Betsey's ear. Desire shivered through her. Little things, like the glint in her eyes, the tilt of her head, the heat of her breath, had that kind of effect on Betsey. Always, in all ways, Jewells could liquefy Betsey's resistance with a simple gesture.

Betsey slowly turned.

"Now untie your top, pretty pretty woman. Untie your top for me."

Dark eyes that could sear, Jewells had. Over

shoulder-length hair tied back, a Panama hat cast a shadow across her face. It didn't matter. Betsey saw her in a spotlight of desire. She saw every freckle, every line, even the twinkle in those fire-starting eyes.

"Like I'm that easy?" Betsey shifted seductively and flirted mercilessly, batting her eyes.

"Well, aren't you?" Jewells tugged at the knot that secured the halter top. *"Aren't you?"* Jewells's finger playfully fluttered on the knot, then the nape of Betsey's neck, then on her shoulder.

"I suppose . . ." Betsey said, as if conceding, but instead she ducked and with a sudden abandon, raced down the beach.

"You just wait till I catch up with you!" Jewells called with a laugh.

Betsey did not turn to see, but she was certain Jewells was right on her heels. Almost within grasp, inches away from capture, Betsey was seconds away from plummeting to the sand in unconditional surrender. Her breathing was ragged, her pants laborious. Her heart beat furiously. *Catch me. Catch me soon!*

Still running, still going, Betsey glanced over her shoulder. But Jewells was not there. Not directly behind her, not farther down the beach, not there at all. The checkered cloth marked the beach like a small red dot. Nothing else.

Betsey slowed to a walk. Her side ached from the unexpected race. A bead of sweat dribbled from her neck toward her halter-covered breasts.

"Yes, okay, I'm that easy," Betsey called to the dunes.

No reply.

"I'm that easy!" Betsey yelled to the ocean.

Nothing.

Betsey untied her top and threw it to the sand. Arms raised to the sky, she danced small pirouettes on the ocean's edge. "Easy. Easy. Easy!"

From out of nowhere, Jewells lifted Betsey, whirling her in a large circle. Around and around they spun — ocean blue spiraled into silver sand into ocean blue into silver sand. Betsey's laughter filled the deserted beach and indignant sea gulls squawked back. Circles into circles into circles until finally, in a dizzy daze, they tumbled to the sand.

"Easy, easy, easy," Jewells mumbled as she kissed Betsey's small breasts.

Betsey opened her eyes to a spinning beach. Above her, the birds reeled in an ongoing oval. "Dizzy," was all she could manage to say.

Jewells pulled her by the hand and they stumbled toward the ocean. Still in her jeans and T-shirt, Jewells didn't seem to care about getting wet. Into the water, waist high, she dragged Betsey.

The ice water raced up Betsey's shorts, across her stomach and lapped her nipples with chilling kisses. Everything tightened in a split second — her nipples crammed into thick pellets, her clitoris compressed into hard-knotted flesh, her skin into teeny goose bumps.

In a blaze, Jewells's hands scorched Betsey's back, challenging the penetrating cold with a sea of fire. Betsey felt her knees buckle and would have faced certain capsize if Jewells hadn't captured her in an overwhelming embrace.

Swallowed in passion, Betsey grabbed Jewells's hair, bit her neck, sucked in her salt-flavored skin.

Marking her desire with desperate, hard kisses, she left a trail of dark welts down Jewells's neck.

Jewells pulled her shirt up and rubbed her firm breasts against Betsey's. Bodies that were cold, yet heated, pressed hungrily into each other. Stiffened nipples strained. Mouths collided.

As if in a race against time, Betsey ripped open Jewells's jeans and reached into her softness. Betsey knew every fold, every crevice. Into slippery flesh, her fingers dove. Jewells' jeans were water-logged, but, even so, Betsey could still differentiate Jewells's own moisture. Betsey slid her finger across the rigid clit and flipped it with fast, hard strokes. Jewells — her face flushed, her breathing quickened — dug her nails into Betsey's shoulders and scraped them harshly down her back. Caressing water suddenly stung.

Jewells began to tremble. Moaning with pleasure, she dragged her nails across Betsey's back once again. The sting caused Betsey to cry out in sweet discomfort. Jewells was shaking. Jewells was shuddering. Her nails dug deeper and deeper. Back and forth, Betsey's fingers swam in Jewells's hidden puddle. Over and over, she fluttered them, until finally, Jewells weakly ran her fingers down Betsey's back one last time.

Standing in the water, surrounded by the unruffled sky, everything became surprisingly calm. Betsey squinted out to the horizon trying to find the precise moment where the ocean touched the clouds.

Softly, Jewells cupped Betsey's face in her hands and brought her from the sky, back to the restless sea. "Forever," Jewells whispered as her sea-wet fingers traced Betsey's lips. "Do you hear me, easy easy girl? I'm in your life forever."

The night air had suddenly become stifling again. Shifting slightly, Betsey gazed out the back of the car. Watching the scenery fade into the night, she searched for the very place the coolness had ended and the humidity began.

"No more lies. I promise," Jewells said, or so Betsey imagined.

Betsey took Jewells's hand. Looking straight ahead, without another word, they drove deeper into the heat.

SOMEWHERE A WITCH

It was a flash downpour from the murky sky that had caused Ryan to duck into the nearest alcove that Thursday afternoon. Colder than she had expected, harder than she anticipated, the rain pounded the pavement. Ryan closed her raincoat and belted it snugly. Four soaking-wet blocks away, her umbrella was locked in the car. Luck had deserted her.

Thick as a gray curtain, the driving rain enclosed Ryan in the awning-covered refuge. Not willing to fight the storm, she leaned against the rough brick wall and waited. The action on the street had quickly subsided. The hurrying passersby, some with newspapers or shopping bags carelessly covering their heads, had disappeared. Traffic slowed to an occasional car or two. Everyone was somewhere, waiting.

Bored with the street's sudden inactivity, Ryan focused on the confines of her dry sanctuary. The soot-blackened brick barely revealed its suffocated, red under-color. The brick wall ended where a dark wooden door began. Nothing had escaped the city's grime. Even the door, showing hints of its once forest-green hue, was now sullied and stained.

An old city, a dirty city — how odd that the rectangular shingle hanging from the doorknob by the shiny silver chain was unscathed. Small brass bells, threaded to the placard's bottom border, tinkled when Ryan tilted the sign. OPEN. The letters were deep purple and painstakingly exact. A spidery design, in the same ink, decorated the upper right and lower left corners.

Ryan glanced to the street which was still bombarded by rain and then back to the elaborate sign. Was this an entrance to a store? She searched for an indication of what lay beyond the door but found nothing. The sign jingled its invitation when she lifted it again.

Ryan twisted the knob and the door creaked open. She peered into the dimly lit hallway which dead-ended into another door less than six feet away. A large sign posted on the door beckoned, YES, WE'RE OPEN, and the pouring rain offered no suggestion of abating. Closing the wooden door behind her, Ryan stepped out of the gray and into the dark.

Undecided about entering, Ryan hesitated when she reached the glass interior door. Black paint completely coated the glass. In thin, uneven letters, the word *Fascinatrix* had been scratched into the paint.

"Still raining?" The glass door jerked open and a rush of air, weighted with a unfamiliar pungent scent, surrounded Ryan. For a brief moment, Ryan's mind somersaulted in the fragrance, unable to completely focus on any one thing. But in another second, the woman in the doorway became crystal clear.

Her hair was as dark as the door's black glass and her eyes, the lashes heavily shaded with thick mascara, were bewitching. She was shorter than Ryan, but her long, wildly tangled hair somehow offered an illusion of height. She wore a black silk dress closed with minuscule rhinestone buttons. From high neck to midcalf, the buttons formed a thin, sparkling line down the center. A black shawl was wrapped low on her shoulders.

The woman opened the door farther, enticing Ryan to step into the candle-lit shop. There were mirrors everywhere. Large and small, they haphazardly covered the walls, hung by purple ribbons from shelves and were scattered randomly on counters. Golden light reflected from every angle. Glass jars lined a counter across the room. Ryan squinted — were those dried flowers stuffed into the containers? Herbs? Sticks? Lining the wall, the shelves were cluttered with half-melted, white candles interspersed with volumes of large books and a collection of various-sized glass panthers.

Flanked by two velvet chairs, a small round table was tucked in the back corner of the room. An ornate black and gold tapestry was draped across the table and hung halfway to the floor. And propped in the center, as though a focal point for the entire room, an extraordinary crystal ball sat.

Ryan's eyes involuntarily fixed on the large globe of glass then drifted to the sinister stand that held it. Intrigued, she took a small step closer. The sphere was perched in the claws of a large black bird that lay frozen on its back. A plastic crow? Ryan inched closer. A wooden hawk? A stuffed, dead raven? The concept of a dead creature, laid on the table, sent a cold chill through her. She could almost hear the ill-fated bird's hideous squawk as it plummeted to the ground.

Yet the crystal ball, so light and airy, provided a brilliant contrast to the ominous bird. Like tiny golden ballerinas, reflected light danced on the orb's curved perimeter. Spinning on the crystal's edge, around and around Ryan they twirled. The dancers, the crystal — slowly the whole room began to rotate.

"Somewhere a witch is combing her hair." The woman's voice cut through the light. In the swirling room, she lifted an antique hairbrush from the seat of the velvet chair.

A witch is combing her hair? Is that what the woman said? Or had she merely stated that *she* had been combing her hair? Ryan felt drugged and confused. The fragrance was too strong, the dancers too fast, the words too slippery.

"An old wives' tale, of course —" The woman continued as she tugged the brush through her blustery hair — "rainstorms being raised by simple acts."

Ryan nodded, wondering if she could sit. The room was becoming a golden blur.

"Are you here for a reading or simply to shop?" the woman asked.

Ryan motioned toward the chair. "I'd like to sit."

"A reading." The woman wrapped her shawl tighter. "Good. It's a perfect day." She took Ryan's hand and led her to the smaller velvet chair. "Some tea? With the rain and the chill ... although you hardly got wet, did you? I'll bring you some tea anyway."

The woman disappeared behind a curtained doorway in the opposite corner. Waiting for her return, Ryan sat motionless. Sitting helped. Her head felt clearer, the room was slowing to a standstill.

Ryan studied the bird that now lay directly in front of her. Its intense, black-bead eye glared and its opened beak was locked in a silent call. Cautiously, Ryan touched the bird. Wood. A sense of relief passed through her. It was a simple, carved black bird, nothing more.

The dizziness had completely passed. After all, it had merely been the onrush of that peculiar scent and the head-spinning lights that had caught her off guard. Ryan glanced briefly at the curtain and then to the crystal ball. A reading? Why not? Her shopping spree had come to a quick halt with the sudden shower. She peered into the glass sphere and saw her inverted reflection gazing back.

I thought so.

Ryan turned to answer the voice but there was no one there. The curtain swayed slightly but the room was empty. Ryan listened hard. There. A voice. From behind the curtain. And another. They were low, almost whispers, then completely silent.

"The herbs are bitter, but sweetened with honey." The woman pushed past the curtain with two cups of tea. "Special herbs, for crystal-gazing."

She placed the steaming cup in front of Ryan. Remaining bits of leaves swirled in the brown brew. "I'm Isobel," she said as she sat in the velvet chair across from Ryan.

Closer, Isobel's features were interesting yet odd. No wonder her eyes had seemed so bewitching at the door. One was a clear, pale blue, the other dark brown. Her nose was straight and her lips, quite thin, had a violet tint. A necklace, made from strands of thin leather, was knotted around her neck and miniature charms — Ryan was uncertain if they were bats or merely birds in flight — dangled from loops in her ear.

"I'm Ryan." Ryan smiled then took a sip of tea. The honey barely covered the bitterness, yet an aftertaste of anise gave the drink a curiously seductive flavor.

"Is the tea okay?" Isobel's gaze was strong, almost as if her contrasting irises were in fierce competition.

"Yes, very good. Thanks."

"When you're done, I'll read the tea leaves in the bottom of the cup," Isobel said nonchalantly, yet Ryan detected a subtle sense of urgency behind the words. Perhaps she had intruded on Isobel? Perhaps

Isobel had friends in the next room — hadn't Ryan heard their voices? — waiting for her return. In a sharp wave of self-consciousness, Ryan finished her tea in several quick gulps.

"Oh, my, that was fast," Isobel laughed. "Well then, let's get on with it." She reached for Ryan's cup and fell into motionless silence. Carefully, she studied the leaves pressed against the delicate china.

"A lizard. Gathering shadows and dreams." Isobel shifted slightly in her chair and peeked from her hooded eyes. "Do you search your dreams?"

Do I what? Ryan thought, but her tongue felt thick, and she couldn't answer.

"It's time to look beyond, into your dreams." Isobel stared into the cup. "There are storm clouds . . ."

Almost deceptively, Isobel's words seemed to slow and Ryan found herself leaning closer, trying to connect each word with the next. But the words soon gelatinized, oozing in molasses-like bubbles from Isobel's plum-tinted mouth.

The room had subtly resumed a snail-paced spin. Ryan grasped the sides of her chair as if, by mere will, she could stop the spiraling. She focused on the tulip-tinted cup in Isobel's long-fingered hands. Had the tea been laced with mind-altering herbs? Drugs? Recklessly, Ryan had gulped the strange brew, only now to consider the unexpected consequences.

Feeling light-bodied yet heavy-headed, Ryan's attention slithered from the cup to the crystal ball. Inside the crystal, she saw herself struggling to unlock her car door. The rain had stopped. As if nervous or perhaps frightened, she hurriedly unclasped her belt and removed her raincoat. Tossing

114

the coat to the back seat, she glanced over her shoulder — once, then quickly again — and jumped in the car and sped off.

"I'm in the crystal," Ryan slurred. Her body seemed to be sliding, her face slowly inching toward the tabletop.

"So . . . you . . . are."

"What?" Ryan could barely lift her head. Cheek pressed against the rough tapestry, she peered into the glass ball. There, in a room that flickered with yellow light, she saw herself with Isobel. How strikingly Isobel's dark, wild hair contrasted with the hooded, white dress she wore.

"Only if you want it." The crystal-held image of Isobel murmured as she circled Ryan in the sphere. Her words flowed almost as softly as the pearl-colored gown she wore.

"I do. I do," Ryan pleaded. She was spinning in circles. From the chair she whirled down, down into the crystal haze.

Isobel stood before her. There were ten, maybe twelve, women in the small room. Dressed in white, they stood in a silent semicircle. No one moved.

An assemblage of candles filled each of the room's four corners. Shadows from objects placed on a large, hand-carved chest danced along the walls. Ryan could discern the silhouette of a chalice and a long knife. A small statue of a voluptuous woman, perhaps a goddess, was centered on the altar. Incense swirled from the icon's arms.

Isobel glanced at Ryan and then at the women. "Then we will cast the circle." As if saluting the sky, she raised the knife above her head and then pointed it to the ground. A woman approached the altar and

115

lifted the chalice. Another removed sticks of smoldering incense from the goddess's arms. Together, the two woman followed Isobel to a corner of the room. Isobel raised the knife again and called out, "Guardians of the East, whose element is Air, we invoke you and call you . . ."

The figures in the crystal shimmered. Ryan closed her eyes, momentarily, to block out the images. Isobel's words were no longer discernible. Something about storm clouds. Something about dreams. So tired, so sleepy, Ryan had to concentrate to force her heavy lids open.

In the crystal globe, the women had formed a circle. She saw herself fall into the crystal and finally come to rest, naked, in the center of a silk-covered table. Refreshingly cool saltwater had been sprinkled across her flesh. A mixture of incense — musk, amber, cinnamon and lemon — wove a thick fragrance in the air. A large white candle flickered at the table's head. The women had joined hands and were breathing in simultaneous deep breaths.

"Blessed Be thy feet. Blessed Be thy knees . . ."

Beginning at Ryan's feet and slowly moving up her body, Isobel dribbled thick oil from a golden vial. "Blessed Be thy breasts. Blessed Be thy lips . . ."

A red candle was offered to Isobel. She anointed it with the oil then held it above Ryan. At the same time, the oil was passed around the circle. Each woman anointed herself, then surrendered the ornate decanter to the next. With soft sighs, the ceremony began.

Someone began a low humming and others joined in. The slow, muffled beat of a drum interwove with the voices, and the humming ripened to a deep-toned chant.

"Candle red as blood, red as fire, ignite desire in our blood."

Isobel tilted the candle and a thin, ruby stream of wax spilled. The wet heat trickled, then pooled to a hot puddle on Ryan's belly. The sweet sting teased her tender flesh and she arched with unexpected pleasure.

Slowly, fastidiously, Isobel dribbled the melted wax across Ryan's small breasts in a series of lines. The entire room seemed to moan each time Ryan arched. Her nipples thickened into plump, brick-red squares. Her hair-hidden sex was sopping with slippery juice. Never had Ryan felt so aroused. The sparking sensations kept her body involuntarily jumping with small, subtle jerks. Liquid heat surged through her veins.

"With a Pentacle of Kisses, I honor Your holiness and offer you my own," Isobel chanted. Her words swirled around the room, rose and fell in soft waves, and seemed to settle back on the five-pointed star of wax that had hardened in thin lines across Ryan's belly and chest.

Women stepped from the dark outskirts of the circle into the center. Ryan's arms and legs were outstretched, forming a human pentacle. The tension from being held apart shot flames of desire throughout her body. Her areolas puckered so tightly that they were no longer distinguishable from the over-erect nipples. Her pussy dripped with quivering anticipation.

The women who held Ryan's limbs began gently kissing her fingers and toes. Kisses melted into licks then back into kisses. Slowly, they inched their way up Ryan's body.

"Blessed Be. Holy One." Isobel passed the candle to a woman. She then raised one hand toward the ceiling and held the other directly above Ryan's throbbing clitoris.

Ryan felt a tingling buzz leap from Isobel's hand to her clitoris. Quickly the sensation increased to a deep vibration. More women moved in from the circle. Ryan's shoulders and hips were pinned to the table. The others continued licking and kissing her arms and legs. Ryan writhed under the restraint.

Someone pulled her pussy lips apart, stretching them wide. Only millimeters away from Ryan's swollen clit-flesh, Isobel held her hand steady. The fast-beating energy whipped around Ryan's clit.

Isobel raised both hands toward the sky. "Blessed Be," she cried.

"Blessed Be," a woman called, then another, then another. The words echoed around the room, weaving a blue glow. "Blessed Be."

Isobel pulled the hood back from her gown and her wild hair tumbled to her shoulders. She tugged the white dress down to her waist, exposing her ample breasts. The sight of the large pale areolas, creased with inverted nipples, fueled the already thundering fire in Ryan's cunt.

Isobel smiled seductively as she flicked her fingertips across her folded nipples. Gradually, the reluctant nipples poked into view. They created a deliciously erotic contrast with the indistinct areolas.

Isobel dropped her gown to the floor and stepped from it. Her waist was small, her hips full. A thatch of untamed curls framed her protruding, chunky clitoris. She climbed onto the table and maneuvered her body until her large clit dangled directly above Ryan's.

"I am Thy fire," Isobel whispered as she anointed Ryan's belly with warmed, scented oil. "I am Thyself." Her strong hands massaged the oil across Ryan's stomach and a breeze of sandalwood, musk and amber encircled Ryan. To her thighs, more oil was spilled; between her cleaved lips, more.

Hands lifted Ryan's ass until her oil-drenched clit lightly kissed Isobel's. A deep, low moan reverberated around the room, leaving an invisible web of endless sound.

Isobel's hips circled as she lowered her thick clit to Ryan's. When the two meaty sex-wedges touched, a streak of lightning jolted the room. Isobel slid her slick, greasy clit across Ryan's and the table began to rock. Fast and desperately, Isobel fucked Ryan's clit with her own. Everything was shaking, rumbling. Earthquakes and firestorms tore down the walls.

Ryan's spirit leapt from her body and sank into Isobel's. For a moment she felt engulfed with flames, then she tumbled back into herself. Again and again, Ryan dove into Isobel and then back. There was nothing but the sea of flaming water.

She was Artemis. She was Diana. She was Aphrodite. She soared like the eagle, descended like the hawk, into Isobel and back. Into Isobel and back.

Isobel slid her fat, rigid clit against Ryan's, over

and over, as melted wax was dribbled across Ryan's rock-hard nipples. Tiny sporadic stings on her breasts tangoed with oozing pleasure from her pussy. A perpetual moaning slammed in tidal waves. Hot rain plummeted. The room flashed with lightning, crashed with thunder, and a storm of purple sparks exploded deep in Ryan's womb.

The angry blare of a car horn caused Ryan to jerk. She was in the street. How she got there, she didn't know. The rain had slowed to a light drizzle yet her hair was wet and her coat was drenched. Her heart was thumping and she was out of breath.

She raced the last block to her car. She felt as if she were being followed, but was uncertain as to why. Even so, she tossed her coat in the back seat, glanced over her shoulder, once, then again, got in the car and locked the door.

The sky suddenly broke into another storm and rain pounded the windshield. Somewhere a witch is combing her hair, Ryan thought vaguely. She started her car and hurried home.

THE CORNER OF
FOURTH AND D

The tattoo parlor's been on the corner of Fourth and D ever since I moved into this ho hum town. Not that that hole-in-the-wall shop made much difference to me — seen one, seen them all. Even so, when the no-action street slumps into its Saturday afternoon stupor, the bench outside Tom's Tattoo is the place to be.

The stream of offbeats that push through Tom's door gives this otherwise pale town some much needed color. On thundering choppers, they roar into town from only God knows where. Most times, they toss me a nod as they pass — like they recognize me from someplace else. They don't. I moved here from upstate a couple of months ago. Doesn't matter, people like us have a natural bent toward one another. When one of them sees one of me, we nod — case closed.

Tom caters to anyone over eighteen but the regulars are Harley-shirted, dirty-jeaned, tough-assed dudes that pull up on their black and chrome cyclones. On occasion, I'll peek in the window and watch Tom zap them. Twice, I've almost gone in myself. Tom's got a wolf sketch on the far wall that would look fuckin' hot on my shoulder, but hell, most Saturday afternoons, after a rough-go week of eight to fives, I've got no real motivation to move from my bench.

Another Saturday, outside Tom's, I was shooting shit with myself and laying low. A bitchin' ruby and gold Harley cut the corner, scorched down the street and came to a dead halt right in front. The leather-clad biker pulled off a black helmet and shot me the nod and a wildfire smile.

In a New York minute, I switched from my standard take five to an upright sit. Her copper-red hair blazed. Her blue eyes were ice. In leather chaps and a silver-studded jacket, she sauntered from the curb, walked past me and disappeared into Tom's. She moved like a panther in heat and I almost fell off the bench as she slinked by.

Her ass, accentuated by the cut-out chaps, was round and full. She had the kind of ass that take-it-easy Saturday women like myself climb off benches and get tattoos for. I was in Tom's before the glass door closed behind her.

"Hey, man, what's happening?" Nonchalant as hell, I nodded to Tom, then headed for the wolf.

In the opposite corner, the woman unzipped her jacket and tossed it across the chair. She wore a thin, low cut T-shirt that blatantly bragged large-nippled breasts.

"Nice jacket," I said, looking at her coat but meaning her tits.

"I know." She propped her foot on the low coffee table and adjusted the strap on her boot.

Messing with her boot, but looking straight at me, her ice-cream-melting smile heated the room. I had a bird's-eye view down her shirt. We both knew it. We both liked it. Apricot-pit nipples on full pert breasts, she was dessert and I was ready to feast.

"You still piercing?" The woman turned to Tom.

"Yeah, but I got a two o'clock." Tom didn't look up from the arm he was tattooing. "Could see you at three."

"No hurry." The woman glanced at the wall clock then flashed her jungle-cat eyes at me. "Nipple," she said as she pulled down one side of her shirt, showcasing her shapely breast. A thick silver hoop, decorated with a lustrous bead, sliced through the ample, pink nipple. "Gonna do the other side. You?"

Her finger playfully fiddled with the silver hoop and her rectangular nipple hardened to a bulky point. My mouth watered and my body throbbed. I motioned toward the wolf but didn't shift my focus from her rosy, erect flesh. "Tattoo."

"Yeah?" Tom said from the corner. "Looking at three-thirty, then."

"No hurry," I muttered.

Did I imagine that she squeezed the swollen tip between her scarlet-nailed fingers before pulling her shirt back in place? Shit. Women like her made me hot as hell.

"Looks like you and me got some time to burn," she said in a sultry voice.

The outline of her popped-hard nipple teased through the flimsy T-shirt. Yeah, I could burn some time with her, all right.

"How 'bout a shot of tequila before Tom gets hold of us. My place is right around the block," I offered, poker-faced, as if I had nothing better to do. Hell, I was dying to get her into my one-room apartment. *Did it hurt when he pierced your nipple?* I'd ask. And she'd lift that lightweight, show-off shirt of hers and dish out her goods for me. *Can I see it again?* I'd ask, almost squeamishly. And damn, that kind of woman — tough as steel — would jump at the chance to strut her macho-femme shit. Her nipple would be between my greedy fingers in seconds.

She grabbed her jacket and followed me out of Tom's. We walked down the street and suddenly this two-bit town seemed to buzz with possibilities. Past the barber's, where old man Joe barely nodded when we cruised by his bench. I felt like we were skating in smooth, gliding steps to my digs.

"They call me Red," she said.

"Red," I repeated. I thought about her pussy hair. I thought about her copper-red snatch. I unlocked the door, tossed a pile of clothes from the chair and headed straight for the tequila.

"And you're . . . ?" Red was walking around the room, checking out my sci-fi books.

"They call me J.C." I handed her a shot glass and we slammed our drinks. Boom. We slammed another.

She flopped in the chair and I sat on the bed. "Nipple pierced, huh," I said, kind of out of the blue. "Did it hurt?"

"Nah, like a hard pinch. Not real bad though." She shifted in the chair as she unzipped her jacket.

I licked my lips then belted another shot. So did she. Boom, boom, boom. "Shit, I can't imagine —"

Bingo. She pulled off her coat and lowered her shirt. "No big deal —" She crossed the room to me. "C'mon, take another look."

"I don't know," I said as I leaned toward the pink square with the silver-beaded hoop.

Inches from my face, she plucked the plump flesh between her painted nails and it swelled to a mouth-watering candy red.

"Is it sensitive to touch?" My words came in hard pants.

She flicked the hoop with her finger then pushed it back and forth in the nipple slit. "Depends" — the s swirled around the room in one long, low hiss — "— on who's touching it." She kneaded the silver bead as she continued to slide the hoop through the tiny pierce.

"Yeah?" I mumbled, hungry as a nipple-crazed newborn.

"Yeah." The word slithered from her mouth.

I nodded like I was agreeing or got the point or

whatever the hell she wanted and Red, like we were clinching a deal, leaned closer. Shit, if she wasn't handing me a blank check, then I don't know what. With one quick lick, my tongue could grab that hoop and tug her nipple straight to my mouth.

"Yeah?" I said again. I clamped my hands on her waist and lassoed my tongue with the nip ring, all in one smooth move.

"Yeah," she moaned.

I sank back on the bed, pulling her by the hoop. She was pushing her puss against my hipbone and growling like a tiger in heat. I played the silver circle with my tongue and she squirmed like she was heading for a fast come-off. Jesus, damn thing sure to hell was fucking sensitive, all right.

I tweaked her fat nipple between my lips and sucked the whole show into my mouth. Her nipple slipped in like an oblong jelly bean. I wrapped the flesh pellet with my tongue and flattened her pink and silver prize against the roof of my mouth.

Red hollered my name, like I was a fuckin' long shot busting ass on the home stretch and she had a couple century notes down. I tried to jimmy my fingers into her tight jeans but she pulled up and started fumbling with my pants, ripping them off like we were racing time.

Red dragged me till my bare ass rode the edge of the bed, then she stood between my dangling legs. "Hot pussy, sweet pussy." She shuffled her words like a Vegas cardsharp. "Hot pussy, sweet pussy. Hot pussy, sweet pussy."

My throbbing pussy was pried open by her fast-paced hands and before I could whisper *Do me good, baby,* she carefully slid one long, thick finger into my slit. Damn, I wanted to suck her whole hand in. I lunged, tempting her into a wild slam but she stuck to her guns, giving me only a slow finger.

"C'mon, baby. C'mon, Red," I begged.

I glanced at my cleaved pussy. She slipped her finger in, real slow, then dragged it to my heavy clit that sprung from my lips like a chunky, plum-colored raisin. In, out, then across the clit, her juice-coated finger glistened.

Red licked the white from her finger and flashed me a slinky smile. "What I like best —" She moved lower between my legs — "about this nipple ring —" She positioned her hooped, bulky nipple above my pussy — "is the things I can do with it."

And then she swooped down, pressing the silver bead against my aching clitoris. The small ball rolled over my clit like a toy steamroller. Red rocked up and down my pussy. The hoop and bead tugged, pressed and hooked my clit-tip which jutted out like a miniature Mt. Everest.

Her nipple and my clit were both knotted and thick — and the little bead kept rolling, the little bead kept pressing. I ran my hands over her chaps. The leather smelled good, smooth to the touch. I closed my eyes and trumped up the scene in Tom's — she had her foot propped on the low coffee table. She was messing with her boot but looking straight at me. Down her shirt, I could see nipples that stuck out like large, salmon-colored squares. I liked her in leather. I liked her hard-ass biker boots.

"Like it, baby?" She swirled the nipple bead faster.

I grabbed her red hair. And her pussy? Was it copper-colored too? I was climbing to a frenzy. I pulled her cunt-flavored tit to my mouth and began to suck. I knew how she liked it. I knew how horny that got her. Flicking the hoop with my tongue, I forced my hand into her pants and down into her glazed heat. She was fuckin' slippery as grease. Yeah, I'd show her finger fucking. Yeah, I'd show her what's what.

She tugged open her pants. Still fluttering that hoop with my tongue, I sunk into her soaking wet entrance. Her fingers found my cunt. I was in hers. We were rolling and rocking and sliding all over the goddamned bed.

The scent of pussy made me crazier. I pushed her from the bed. "Stand for me, Ms. Leather-ass."

She stood in the center of the room, jeans opened, shirt bunched around her waist and smirked like the macho-femme she thought she was. I lunged for her and we slammed to the floor. I undid her chaps, pulled her pants down to her don't-fuck-with-me boots and plunged my tongue into her bronze-tinted mane.

While I gave her my best, she reached for the bottle of tequila and took another slug. She grabbed me by the hair and pulled my face from her *chacha* then took another swig. "Do me with the bottle," she said with a nasty grin.

I took the bottle from her, chugged a couple myself and spread her rough-and-ready pussy open. Real easy, I poked the lip of the bottle into her wrinkled opening. Her pussy rim popped around the banded top. A perfect fit. Nice and easy, I screwed the bottle in and out of her steamy flesh. The red-haired cream pie took as much as I could give. The stem of the bottle was slathered in milk-white sex dew. I slammed another drink, licking the come from the glass as I did.

She took the bottle from me and pushed it back in. She fucked herself with the bottle and rammed her finger across her swollen wedge of flesh, in sync. Offering a helping hand, I poked my thumb into her tight asshole. Past the tip of my finger, till the entire nail disappeared, I burrowed into her chute. Her eyes flashed with the pleasure of pain and she started to pop off hard.

The sight of her pussy swallowing the bottle, her engorged, flushed clit being strummed nonstop, the pulsating of her ass crevice on my large thumb — I reached my limit. I sliced my finger against my clit and together we blew.

It wasn't that big of a deal watching Tom pierce Red's other nipple. She grimaced and whimpered but the look in her eyes was the very same look I had seen only twenty minutes earlier when I had pushed my thumb into her ass. All the same, I nixed the wolf tattoo. After all, there'll be plenty of slow Saturdays when there'll be nothing better to do on the corner of Fourth and D. I'll get my tattoo then.

BOBBY'S GIRL

"Did you let him kiss you?" Kerry whispered.

An awkward silence veiled the already darkened bedroom. Kerry, next to Devon in the crowded twin bed, momentarily held her breath. A simple yes from Devon would put a million miles between her best friend and herself, of this she was sure. At thirteen, she wasn't allowed to wear lipstick, let alone meet a boy at the park. Yet Devon had just admitted that she and Bobby McQuire had spent over an hour together, after sunset, at Lawson Park.

"You *promise* you won't tell?" It wasn't so much

130

Devon's words as her tone that skidded to a screeching halt in the pit of Kerry's stomach.

They had kissed, of course they had kissed, Kerry thought dismally. Alone in the park with a boy, Lady Pink lipstick on her never-been-kissed lips, Devon had only done what any other of the girls would have done, given the chance.

"Cross my heart," Kerry whispered. She clenched her fists, bracing herself for the worst. Once a girl has kissed a boy, she's likely to forget her best friends — so Mary Beth Landers, the new girl from Claremont Junior High, had disclosed to Kerry at lunch last week.

"He wanted more than a kiss," Devon confided.

"More?" Morbid curiosity overshadowed the fear of abandonment Kerry had harbored only moments before. She shifted toward Devon. "Did you do more?"

Devon twisted beneath the lightweight quilt to face Kerry and whispered in her ear, "He tried to unzip my pants."

Kerry was uncertain if it was Devon's musk perfume or the sudden image of her own hands unzipping Devon's pants and sliding into Devon's secret place that set in motion a hard tingling between her own legs. She discreetly squeezed and released her thighs, as if that private movement could somehow alleviate the building pressure. *Did you let him?*"

"We were at the park. Bobby said he knew a special place, over near the pond . . . you know where that path leads into the woods? We went a little ways into the trees. There was this place, not too far, but hidden away. It was really pretty —"

Anticipating the details of Devon's confession, Kerry lay quietly in the darkness. Like a slow-motion video, her often fantasized, heat-inciting scenario of her own thick finger easing into Devon's softness played before her closed eyes. How desperate her anxious finger was to slip into Devon's juicy folds! Kerry knew, all to well, about the wetness — so often at night, alone and bored — she'd slither her own flesh-hungry finger into her lacy panties. She would nudge and stir the flaccid hump of skin, first luxuriating in the sensations and then tracing her damp fingertip beneath her nose.

She had often wondered about Devon. Was she also wet down there? Did she also smell so sweet? Kerry's breath quickened at the thought. She crossed her legs tightly as the tingling pushed into a constant ache.

"Bobby said he loved me and then..." Devon paused, as if for effect, "...he kissed me." Her words cascaded like a waterfall.

"Did you like it?" Kerry asked. Her need to know warred with her growing, stomach-turning fear. She wished Devon would get to the point.

A brief silence rolled across the room like a morning fog before Devon spoke. "It was okay." Her sultry tone bubbled like a slow boil, vaporizing the cool quiet. "But then, *you* wouldn't know, *you've* never been kissed," Devon pointed out, as though she were now a much envied woman of the world.

"So, big deal!" Kerry snapped, not bothering to hide her sarcasm.

"I didn't mean it like that," Devon said apologetically. "What I meant was —"

"That I'll never know till I get kissed," Kerry

moaned. "Which will be forever. I can't wear lipstick. I'm not allowed at the park with a boy. I'll be twenty-five before I ever get a chance!"

"Hmm," Devon said in agreement.

Although disappointment edged her voice, in reality, a kiss from a boy was the last thing Kerry wanted. Her true desires centered around impressing Devon. Frustrated, Kerry stared at the thin line of light that outlined the bedroom door. Now that Devon had ventured this far with Bobby, Kerry suspected that Devon would soon lose interest in her. Devon was on the verge of disappearing forever into the complex world of boys. An empty despair consumed Kerry. She'd soon be left behind.

As if sensing Kerry's concerns, Devon suddenly exclaimed, "I know, I could show you. I'll pretend that I'm Bobby and you can be me." Devon climbed out of bed and clicked on a small lamp. A low, golden glow dimly lit the room. She locked the door, fumbled through her purse then pulled out a dark tube of lipstick.

"Here. Lady Pink." Devon hurried to Kerry who sat cross-legged in the middle of the bed. She painted the lipstick on Kerry's mouth. "Oh, you look *so* pretty in this color."

Kerry ran her tongue across her lips which now felt fuller, plusher and more glamorous than ever before. Why had she been so afraid? Devon — a good friend, the best of friends — would never desert her. The emptiness dissipated and Kerry smiled seductively. "Am I pretty enough for a kiss, Bobby?"

Devon laughed. "The prettiest!" She clicked off the light, pulled the blanket, tent-like, over both herself and Kerry and snuggled close. "Bobby put his arms around me, like this," Devon said as she tenderly wrapped her arms around Kerry. "And then he said, 'I love you.'"

The blanket removed any remnants of light that had filtered into the room from beyond the door. In the enveloping blackness, Devon ran her fingers through Kerry's shoulder-length hair. "I love you," she said softly, lightly kissing Kerry on the cheek.

Kerry couldn't help but wonder if Bobby had truly meant those cherished words, or if, as Mary Beth had cautioned, they were "just the way boys got what they wanted from girls." Had he said "I love you" as affectionately as Devon just had? Had the closeness poured from him like it now did from Devon?

"I love you," Devon whispered again. Her warm breath caressed Kerry's ear.

"You do?" Kerry was uncertain if she was playing Bobby's girl or Devon's.

"Yes, I do." Devon's words were muffled as her lips tentatively touched Kerry's.

Devon's lips were so soft, so warm and sweet. Devon's fingertips — as they traced her ear, her cheek, her neck — left a tiny trail of sparks. Devon's perfume saturated the air. The sound of her sighs filled the silence. Under the blanket, Kerry's senses were flooded with Devon.

Devon teased Kerry's lips with her tongue and then pressed for entry. Mary Beth Landers had talked about frenching, all the girls had, and when Devon's tongue teased Kerry's mouth, Kerry didn't resist.

"He kissed me like this," Devon said faintly. Her breathing had taken on a slightly erratic quality.

Kerry was silent. The image of her finger separating Devon's cleaved flesh once again shot through her mind. Her breathing shifted to a quick pant.

Devon's hand slid beneath Kerry's T-shirt. Gently, she rubbed her finger from nipple to nipple. Like a closed circuit, the electric throbbing skipped from between Kerry's legs to her nipples then back. Scattered waves of pleasure radiated throughout her body.

Kerry focused on the vivid picture of her finger sliding like a snake through Devon's flaxen hair, into the pink — all the way to the opening. She could think of nothing else. Moisture seeped from her slit and soaked her panties. If she were to put her own finger down there — or better yet, if Devon were to — it would be slick, it would be gooey and the air beneath the blanket would churn with her scent.

Devon's hand stretched the elastic band on Kerry's panties, stole across her belly, and stopped at the fringe of hair. "And then he —"

Shut up about him! Had she actually said those words? Her heart pounded wildly. The hardened area between her legs pulsated at the same crazed pace. There was no room left for Bobby, not under this blanket, not between Devon and her — no room anywhere.

Devon eased her finger into Kerry's petaled-flesh and held it still. "I wish that I could see what —"

"You could look," Kerry interrupted, desperately. "Get the flashlight."

Devon flipped the blanket off and reached for the same flashlight they had earlier used to read Bobby's secret notes to Devon. Back under the blanket,

Devon clicked on the light. A damp spot saturated the crotch of Kerry's panties and light blond curls struggled with the binding elastic. Devon pulled the panel of cotton aside and exposed Kerry's dangling, rose-tinted clitoris.

It seemed like forever that Kerry had waited, and so patiently at that, to say what she next said. Almost gasping from excited anticipation, she glanced down at her spotlighted, sopping vulva. "Did he unzip your pants?"

Devon looked her straight in the eye and shook her head.

A hurricane of relief and exhilaration spun through Kerry. He hadn't unzipped her pants. Of course not! An act so personal was reserved for only the closest of lovers, wasn't it? "He didn't," Kerry said, more than asked.

Devon giggled.

"Let's pretend . . ." Devon whispered, ". . . that he did." She dipped her fingers — not one, but two, between Kerry's oily lips, hesitated momentarily, then pried into the small, red-rimmed entrance.

A hot fire flared in Kerry's vagina and she whimpered. Devon's fingers seemed to dig into her tight crevice. The pleasure burned. It was too much. It was too good. Less but more, slow but fast — the contradictions of sex rode her hard. Giving in, she pushed herself farther onto Devon's hand.

The flashlight fell to the bed. Kerry stopped rocking on Devon's hand, reached for the light and aimed it between Devon's legs. She desperately wanted to see what Devon looked like — after all, she had spent so many hours, alone in bed, wondering about her best friend. Kerry pulled the cotton panty aside. Devon's sex was concealed beneath a thicket of hair. Kerry spread the thin lips and studied the small, dark flange of flesh. Creamy drops frosted the hanging, pink lower flaps.

Cautiously, Kerry fingered Devon's clitoris and then slid toward the place that Bobby hadn't been allowed to venture. Devon smiled the most beautiful smile and nodded. Kerry could barely contain the elation that surged through her as she slid her finger into the sweetened pot.

Devon resumed moving her fingers in and out of Kerry. On and on, over and over, they strummed each other's pleasure points. The sensations mounted, then subsided; mounted and subsided until finally, as each of the girls beat their fingers in relentless, fast-paced circles, they both collapsed in shuddering release.

The room fell into a delicious silence. Kerry clicked off the flashlight and the darkness returned. Cradled in Devon's arms, she let out a relaxed sigh, no longer worried about Bobby — or anyone else. Once a girl had kissed her best friend, she was likely to forget about boys.

CHARISMA

The door clicked open and in she swished. The first thing I noticed after the knee-knocking whirlwind of exquisite perfume? Her taste for pricey men's clothes. The shoes — had to be Charles Jordan. Buffed to a deluxe shine, they squeaked with each step across the linoleum floor. She wore an oversized suit, black with a fine gray pinstripe, decked with a burgundy tie and Cartier tie tack. When she pushed the door closed, a glimpse of her diamond-studded Rolex flashed beneath her jacket cuff. Topping her mahogany-colored hair, a classy Stetson wrapped the package. Her preference for the masculine look did justice to her slender, feminine frame. She was a high-rent doll, dressed uptown. Like a Ralph Lauren model on a Paris runway, she did a graceful, sweeping half-turn, then slinked into the chair across from my desk. Nice. Real nice.

It had been a long time since anything interesting had come through my door. All I'd done the last few months was insurance company investigations. Sure, rent got paid, but sitting with a camera outside some bozo's house, day after day, waiting to see if the too-injured-to-work party forgets he's hurt and lifts a garbage can or suitcase or God knows what, is slow-cooked cash.

I studied the beaut across from me and gave her a half-nod. "Ms. Sheridan?"

"Nikki," she replied. She glanced at the wall behind me, maybe eyeballing my diploma or sizing up the books on the cluttered shelves.

"Nikki," I repeated. I doodled the letter N on the pad in front of me.

"I'm so glad you were able to see me on such short notice. Beverly Martin, a dear friend of mine, works at Principal. She gave me your name." Nikki's gaze diverted back to the shelves. "I've never... This is so awkward, really... It's just that I need to have someone..." Her sentences were stacking like uneven dominos.

"Been cheated on?" I said, matter of fact. After three years in the business, I had a nose for these things.

Like azure darts, her eyes shifted to mine. She clicked open her small clutch and pulled out a gold cigarette case. "Do you mind?"

Before she had time to bat an eye, I fired her cigarette with my Zippo. I had no doubt that this lady was used to the best.

She took a slow drag then exhaled dramatically. "Women *don't* cheat on me," she said coolly.

Women, huh. I wouldn't have guessed she was the type. Hell, I'd had a taste of that kind of honey a time or two myself. And looking at the sweets sitting across from me, I had an itch to change my diet back to desserts. But after last year's fiasco, I don't dip my pen in company ink, I don't mix my business with my pleasure, and I stay away from glamour girls with problems. Period.

I gave Nikki a street-smart, not-tempted smile. "Then what is it that they do that's brought you to me?"

She took another long drag. "There's a woman who's come into my life. I need to know —" A drawn-out exhale. "— if she's who she says she is."

"Is this business or romance?" I cut right to the chase.

The classy woman shot me a nickel-and-dime smile and crushed her smoke into the Howard Johnson's ashtray on the edge of my desk. "Her name is Christina York, although some call her Tina. We're starting a business together."

"So you want a financial background?" Easy enough, I thought.

"I've fallen in love with her," Nikki continued, as if I hadn't spoken. "I'd give her anything she wanted. She's that dear to me. It's just that . . ." She fiddled with the swan-shaped catch on her clutch. "I've only known her a couple of months. She's wonderful, really, more than I could have ever dreamed. It's just that something's not quite right."

Her tone had softened. She sounded twelve, maybe thirteen. The swan clicked open then shut, open then shut. Nikki stared at the shelves behind me. She seemed a million miles away.

"Fallen in love." I figured a quick recap would bring her back from the fantasyland she'd drifted off to. "And you want me to check her out."

Nikki refocused her attention on me. The tough edge that had veiled her eyes returned. "Discreetly, of course. Christina would be terribly hurt if she had any inkling of my distrust. She bases so much on loyalty." Long pause. "*My* loyalty."

Loyalty. I haphazardly scribbled the word beneath the uneven row of *N*s. Nikki was my kind of girl, faithful but not blind.

"So what's set off the alarms?" I asked, reaching for my lighter. She had pulled out another smoke.

"It started when Christina's aunt had a sudden stroke. It was the night before we were to meet with Alex Stroden from National Bank. Christina fell apart. She was close, very close to her aunt. She raised her. Christina's mother ran off when Christina was twelve, never to be seen again."

According to Nikki, after Christina had returned from her aunt's, she made a reference to her mother. Because of the aunt's illness, Christina had to take over payments on her mother's house and wouldn't be able to cosign a loan with her.

Nikki's voice raised an octave. "I said, 'Your *mother's* house? I thought she disappeared years ago.' Not an issue, really. There were plenty of reasonable explanations. Well, Christina came up with one. But it's odd. As she told me this long, involved story about her mother leaving this house behind, on and on, there was something in Christina's eyes that betrayed her words."

I nodded. I'd seen liar's eyes — cool, direct, but subtly vague. "And the loan at National Bank?"

"The aunt died a few days after Christina's return. Christina was a wreck. Everything was in upheaval. I shrugged off my uneasiness about things and went ahead with the loan, in my name only. I thought getting the business started would help pull Christina from her depression — which indeed it did."

Nikki ran her red fingernail across the desk. The scratching sound broke the sudden silence. She exhaled and a rush of cigarette smoke surrounded me. The familiar urge to light one up tugged heavily then fizzled. I still kept one last emergency smoke next to my lighter in my desk. I'd quit three long weeks ago, and not an hour went by that I didn't open the drawer, at least once, and rerun my choice.

"Although I had the credit and start-up funds to carry the business loan myself, I had wanted Christina's participation, more as a show of commitment than anything else. But she was so caught up in her aunt's death . . ." Nikki took another drag. "The business has started. Christina and I are together." She clicked the pocketbook twice. "It's just that something's not quite right. There are discrepancies — minor, silly things." That same adolescent vulnerability shadowed her face. "When I ask her, or try to talk to her about inconsistencies — what she's said or done — she gets that look in her eyes. That look of betrayal." Nikki paused and gazed into fantasyland before adding, "Christina dazzles. She has a charisma, a certain style, that's impossible to resist."

"You want me to find out about Christina," I reiterated, making sure I was closing a deal with the adult Nikki, not the love-struck adolescent dreamer.

"Yes." Nikki's eyes narrowed and her tone hardened. She crushed the second cigarette into the cheap glass ashtray and seared me with her gaze. "Everything."

Christina worked out at Isis, a women's gym in the Valley, three evenings a week. From seven-thirty until closing, Christina made a point of keeping in shape, rain or shine, tired or not — or so Nikki told me.

Ready for action in my workout duds, I sat on an exercise bike waiting for her to strut through the door. What she had going for her that had melted Nikki, I couldn't fathom. The photo showed a tough-ass woman sporting an attitude-laden smile. Slicked-back, black hair and beady, brown eyes, she looked like trouble with a capital *T*. Sure, her aunt had died and poor, grief-stricken Christina was too heartbroken to sign the loan papers. Yeah, yeah, spare me the sob story. As far as I was concerned, this case was open and shut.

Monday, Wednesday and Friday, I sat at the gym and waited. No Christina. When I relayed this news flash to Nikki, she swallowed it like a baby does castor oil.

"She *said* she was going to the gym," Nikki said,

a tinge of disbelief graying her words. "Why would she lie about that?"

"Beats me." Trouble with a capital *T*. "Double-check and get back to me."

Confused, Nikki returned my call. She had put the screws on Christina whose comeback was some convoluted spiel about last-minute changes. "I told you I had other plans," Christina had charged. "Why don't you pay attention to me anymore?"

"I must have crossed wires or misunderstood Christina's plans," Nikki later argued.

"Yeah, maybe," I said sarcastically.

Another client that I'd have to spoon-feed the truth. Even though Nikki had hired me, the situation wasn't that simple. Bottom line: Nikki wanted to believe Christina. I'd seen this same song and dance a million times. I'm hired to do a run-of-the-mill character check and my client, riddled with disbelief, fights me all the way. Every double-cross I uncover is counteracted by hope-saturated excuses, straight from the paying party's mouth. Makes no sense to me.

But underneath her love-fogged P.O.V., Nikki must have known, as all my clients know, that the sweetheart in question was probably a bad apple. No matter how rosy the skin, you can only hide spoiled goods for so long. That's why, amid all the squawking, and the *maybe this* and *maybe that* excuses, the investigation was still a go. In spite of Nikki's ongoing whitewash, I went to that gym, as requested, three nights a week, for two weeks straight, until Christina finally showed.

* * * * *

"Hey, how ya doing!" Her words lit up the entire room. Friday night, seven-thirty, it was just me on the bike and the trainer behind the desk when the door flung open and Christina breezed in.

"Hey, Tina, long time," the trainer said. The sparkle in her eyes suggested they were more than mere acquaintances. Much more.

The trainer leapt over the low counter and surrounded Christina in a bear hug. Christina returned her hug with a playful push and a fast punch. Their mock fight ended with deep laughs and Christina headed for the locker room.

I climbed off the bike and headed toward the lockers.

"How ya doing?" Christina greeted me as I pushed past the curtain.

"Fine, thanks." Bullshit. I was damn tired of exercising. I grabbed a towel and flung it around my neck.

"New around here?" Christina pulled her sweatshirt over her head and her sweat pants down.

We both checked out her reflection in the full-length mirror. In a tight tank top and loose-legged shorts, she looked pretty damn good. The closest I'd ever been to a buffed-to-the-max woman was to hold a *Muscle and Fitness Magazine* in the late P.M. Yeah, yeah, I masturbate to Ms. Olympia, big deal.

"You must come here often," I said. Admiration pumped my words.

"Three times a week, rain or shine," Christina boasted.

Double bull shit, I thought, but tossed her an appreciative smile.

"Tina," the trainer called from out front. "Phone."

"That's me, see ya." Christina tossed her sweats and bag in a locker, clicked the lock shut and headed out.

Was that Nikki on the phone, checking up on Christina? I figured I should tune in, just in case. I gave myself a onceover in the mirror. Flexed my arms — not bad. Checked my ass — not bad. Something about Christina made me want to look my best.

"Sure, baby, see ya then." Christina hung up the phone, gave the trainer a swat on the ass and started doing stretches.

Too long in front of the locker room mirror, I had missed the conversation. Sleeping on the job, son of a bitch. I climbed back on the exercycle and gave a nice, easy pedal. Christina swaggered to the free weights and picked up a laden barbell. My arms ached just from watching her do her reps. I kept tabs on her reflection in the mirror. She had a look on her face that could bring babies to tears. Her biceps bulged. Her triceps inflated. She was dripping sweat before I'd reached one-half mile.

She looked good. There was a hell of a lot more to Christina than that big zero photo Nikki had pawned off on me. Her thighs were rippled steel. Her calves were bulked muscle. A killer ass, a flat belly. Sure, I'd had a happening or two with women in the past, but never, ever, a woman like Christina.

Christina flexed. Incredible. I licked my lips and pedaled. She squatted, spread her legs and tightened her thighs. Beads of sweat dripped from my forehead. I pedaled and pedaled and pedaled. I was flying in the Tour de France. Two miles? Five miles? Ten miles? Heading toward Christina, I raced for the finish. I was soaked. Sweat poured down my neck and pooled around my waistband. I'd have to ask Nikki for a better photo. A picture with more detail, with more substance. I needed something I could show around, sink my teeth into. I needed more.

"You really push on that cycle." Somehow Christina had sneaked behind me and thrown me off guard.

I was drenched. Sweat gathered in small puddles on the floor. "Yeah, I like a good workout," I said, real nonchalant, although I knew I probably wouldn't be able to walk for a month.

"I like a woman who takes her body seriously," she said in a low voice.

Her tone was heated. She stood close to me, so close that I could smell the scent of her pumped up body. *This is how she smells during sex,* I thought hungrily.

"Good," I said, uncertain why. Business was suddenly feeling way too pleasurable. I climbed off the bike. I needed some space, ASAP, between me and Christina.

With a fast laugh, Christina slapped me on the back and headed for the leg press. Overtaken by a rush of her head-spinning scent, I stood by the bike and stared.

Except for the small light on the nightstand, the

room was dark. Flopped on the bed, unable to bend my legs, I let out a moan. Punished by a body that was pissed as hell, I had chewed myself out the entire drive home. In one short hour, I had blown a two-week scam. I had my subject right in the palm of my hand and I had scored one unbelievable lead: *how she'd smell during sex.* I had diddled away time like a goddamn greenhorn.

Not until I got home and unpacked my gym bag did I stumble on my lucky break. On the sly, good ol' Tina had dealt me in the game. A note — signed, sealed and delivered — was stuck inside my shoe. She must have tagged it while I was showering. *Pleasures Unlimited. Saturday night, 11:00 PM. Would love to see you there, Tina.* An address was scribbled on the back.

The dime-a-dozen photo of Christina lay on the nightstand. I tilted it against the base of the lamp and gave her a last onceover. She stared back at me with her tough-ass smirk. I clicked off the lamp and lay there in the dark, a smile plastered on my face. This was my kind of case.

It had been a good night. Christina was where I wanted her. With a little fancy footwork, she'd be eating out of my hand. The potential coup de grace tasted sweet. *Pleasures Unlimited?* Not a night club. Hell, I knew the joints in this town, straight and gay, like the back of my hand. Not in the phone book, not listed anywhere — yeah, I had my questions about Pleasures Unlimited, all right. And I had five bucks that said Nikki would have her share of questions, too.

My opinion. Christina was doing Nikki wrong. For her money? For a free ride? For the game? Hard to figure. But I'd check out the landscape and paint a portrait that would put Van Gogh to shame. And after I cracked this case into a thousand double-crossing pieces, not only would I have a sweet bank roll in my pocket, but also a broken-hearted, well-dressed, money-to-burn Nikki crying in my more-than-understanding arms. Business was looking up.

Later that night, I awoke in the back seat of a hard-driving dream. My hand was jammed between my legs. How it got there, I don't know. But there it was, crammed in my boxers, drenched in sex juice. The room was dark and that hot, sweet, unforgettable scent — *how she smells when she has sex* — was all over me like French perfume. I was soaked in sweat, hers and mine.

She had climbed into my dream, oh yes, oh yes, with her ready-for-action, powerhouse arms. She turned on the lamp, pulled the blanket off me and brushed her tight chest across mine.

I don't mix business with pleasure, I said point-blank.

This isn't business, she said, real cocky.

I had to consider. After all, I had already punched out on Nikki's time clock hours before.

"No," I said again, but the look I gave her told the truth. I wanted it from her and I wanted it hard. I had seen her in the gym. I knew how many reps she could do. Over and over, she could keep it going. Iron biceps, steel thighs — no man or woman had ever caught my attention like Christina.

"No?" She'd been around the block a few times. She knew the ropes. With a fast tug, she grabbed both my hands and held them against the headboard. "No?"

I shook my head. A rough burning radiated from where her hand was clenched. I liked the way it ached.

"So what's the story, P.I.?" Still clutching my wrists, her other hand pushed back and forth across my naked breasts.

Small and red, my nipples stood stiff. Christina plucked the erect flesh between her fingers and hot desire bull's-eyed my cunt. She pinched, she squeezed the hard stubs. Yelping like a puppy, I squirmed beneath her. Her pussy slammed against mine as she rotated her hips like there was no tomorrow.

She kissed me and kissed me like I've never been kissed — like she was trying to climb all the way inside of me, and if she pushed hard enough, she might go all the way to my soul. Her lips were hard and soft, all at once, and I sucked them into my mouth. Sucked them like she was mine, like I was hers. Her mouth ended where mine began. There was no separation.

I pressed my tits against hers. Her body was warm, solid, smooth. She stayed on top, took control and began to touch me like I'd never been touched. Christina was a take-charge woman — a new, delicious experience for a jaded gal like myself. Sure, I'd rolled with a few on-the-bottom femme types and plenty of wake-me-when-it's-over dudes, but never had it been like this.

Her fingers went from tit to tit as she kissed my

cheeks, my neck, my chest. She sucked a path of purple hickeys from my breasts to my belly. Down she slid. She licked, she bit, she painted me with her tongue.

Her muscular arms pinned my legs apart. My clit, like a ripened berry, hung swollen and wet. Hungry for the feel of her thick fingers up my slit, her tongue on my pussy, I split my lips open for her.

Christina moaned. "Want me to suck it big, baby?"

I fingered my pussy. No way it could get any bigger than it already was. I stretched the lips tighter. The flesh hood pulled back and the domed clit jutted into full view.

"Yeah, baby!" Christina exclaimed. She tossed me a hard, sexy smile and then buried her face in my cunt.

Flexed to a point, her tongue pushed and prodded. She kneaded up and down the side of the shaft then flicked across the clit-tip itself. Unbearable rushes crashed through me in thick, fast waves.

I was sopping. I couldn't hold myself tight enough apart. She couldn't pin my legs far enough. Tension spiraled into tension. I moved my hips in a desperate grind. She dug her hands into my ass cheeks and propped me higher. Sweat poured from me, dripped from her. The room smelled like Christina smells when she has sex.

Cruising in the back seat of my dream, I pounded my hand back and forth in my boxer shorts. The bed was soaked with my sweat, our sweat. Christina did it good. Christina did it hot.

And God, she was all over me. All over me, all over me, all over me.

Saturday morning, it took two cups of coffee, a shower, and four squirts of cologne to shake the creepy feeling that Christina had actually been in my bed the night before. Sure, at three A.M., alone and aroused, the fantasy had been worth a nice, long look-see. But next morning, until I was plugged all the way in, her telltale scent still followed me from room to room.

Like some kind of a fool, I washed my face twice again and sprayed extra cologne, just in case. Not until I settled down with a glass of juice and a buttered bagel did I take a moment to recap the crazy morning ritual I had put myself through. My ridiculous behavior stung like a slap in the face. Even so, Christina's photo seemed to have propelled that tough-ass smirk from the bedroom nightstand to the living room wall. No matter how much I washed, how much cologne I doused myself with, the stinking fact remained — Christina was still all over me.

Desperate for distraction, I scribbled on the note pad in front of me. A sudden compulsion to expose the spoiled spot on this rotten apple, PDQ, swept through me. With a precise game plan and some smart legwork, Christina would be one less bad apple in the barrel.

I doodled a row of Ns. The image of Nikki, dressed to kill, materialized. She paced across my living room. Her hair, no longer pinned beneath a hat, cascaded in rich brown curls around her creamy complexion. Occasionally she'd glance at me with her lake-tinted eyes. Those cool blues could stir red heat, I had no doubts about that.

The low-cut green dress she wore spilled across her heavenly curves like liquid emeralds. Not hidden beneath baggy men's trousers or a too-long suit coat, her hips swished and swayed. And her breasts, fuller than I would have wagered, pressed desperately against the sequined, green material.

With the intensity of a caged tigress, Nikki crossed the room. Smooth and sleek, back and forth, she moved in front of me. The breeze of her perfume did a nonstop swirl.

Overnight, my bedroom, my living room — my goddamn condo — had become a playground for mind trips. Eyes closed, I did a fast one-two shake of the head, trying to chase away the vision. But the constant swish as she moved from the oriental rug to the hardwood floor and back continued.

Then it was quiet. I opened my eyes for a quick peek. Nikki had stopped pacing. She was across from me in the leather recliner. Her dressed was hiked and the dark border of her stockings caught my eye. Her cream-colored thighs were neck and neck with the lacy black garter straps for my attention.

"I don't know what I would ever have done without you," Nikki murmured.

I struggled to focus my rebel eyes on her face. Her succulent lips were painted pale pink. Did that salmon shade match the color of her pussy? My gaze recklessly leaped to her thighs.

"I owe you so much," Nikki whispered. She uncrossed her legs, as if oblivious to the gift she offered. I had a sudden view up her shiny, emerald dress. Part of me hoped for panties — nothing like a line of thin, lacy material stretched tight across a bulging, fat snatch. All the same, no panties meant a possible shot of her pussy hair. Hell, if I was lucky enough, perhaps I'd even get a glimpse of the pink stuff.

"You cracked the case *so* quickly," Nikki said. She separated her legs and indiscreetly exposed her thatch.

"Just a couple lucky breaks." I swallowed hard. Lady Luck, don't leave me now, I prayed.

"It's hard to face the truth about Christina..." She leaned back in the recliner, seemingly unaware that her legs had spread further and her pussy lips had sliced apart. She kicked off her green high heels, then rested her feet on the edge of the chair.

Redder than her pale pink lipstick had suggested, her bulky clit was in full view. In frantic response, my clitoris began to pound. Saliva seeped into my mouth. My breathing switched to a short, quick series of exhalations.

"The truth is always best," I muttered, weighing heavily a sudden urge to drop to the floor and do a fast crawl to the foot of her chair.

"Yes, I suppose." Her legs eased further apart and her entire honey-dip was mine for the asking. "You really like your work, don't you?"

Like my work? Like my work? What wasn't to like?

"Suppose so," I muttered, staring point-blank at her cherry-colored bundle. With a deep breath, I nose-dived to the floor and raced like a baby derby winner to the sweet finish.

"Don't deny me, baby. Don't deny me." Between

her legs, sucked into the mouth-watering scent of her voluptuous pussy, I pleaded.

"Why," she exclaimed delightfully, "I would have never guessed —"

Never guessed what? That I would crawl across the floor to bury my face in her pussy? That I would lift her legs on my shoulders and burrow in as far as I could?

From across the room, her pussy had looked mink-covered, but close up, it was a mere, but ample, strip of hair that covered her otherwise shaved triangle. Her abundant clit was fringed with flapping lower lips. They were so large that unless I tugged them aside, her slit would remain completely under wraps. No way. I pinched the dangling flesh between my fingers and opened them wide. Home run. Her slit was red-rimmed and ready for action. Her secret juice pooled in the pink cradle.

Why the hell it had been so long since I'd had a woman, I couldn't fathom. Didn't matter anymore. I was on my way back to paradise. I slammed two fingers in and her pussy walls clamped me like there was no tomorrow. Like she was doing some kind of gymnastic stunt with her cunt, she held me firm. *How's that?* I crammed in another. She gripped tighter. *And that?* Four fingers in and slippery come started greasing my entire hand.

"Give it all to me. Give it all to me," Nikki moaned.

More than four? What else could I do but try to please the lady?

Her stronghold on my dripping wet fingers suddenly loosened — there was plenty of room in her ready-for-action pussy. She swiveled her hips in fast circles as I pushed in deeper. I tucked my thumb as best I could — the only thing I could figure was to try to make a fist. I pressed on. She yelped. I backed off. She cried no.

"Okay, baby," I said. I was giving her one last chance to come to her senses.

"Hard. Slam me hard with all of it."

Who would have guessed that Ms. High-Rent Nikki would want it this way? Boom, I rammed in. Her slit took my whole hand, swallowed it right up. Then she started rocking, she started jamming.

I did what I figured she was asking for. Over and over, I gave her the fist. She was jumping around like a fish on sand — moaning and crying and calling my name. I fucked her hard. I did it like a pro until she squirted — and I mean squirted — wet come all over my recliner.

The vision of Nikki had done a vanishing act and I was staring, like a kid at a pet shop window, at an empty leather recliner. My eyes felt like the lids had been propped open for the last half hour and my mouth was bone dry. The goddamn place was haunted.

I glanced from the leather recliner back to the row of Ns I had doodled and forced myself to blink. Nikki. Nikki. Nikki. Glamour girls with problems — a tough habit to break.

After struggling with my street map, I finally

pinpointed the locale of Pleasure Unlimited, near the pier, in a questionable part of town. It was early afternoon. The street was deserted except for a couple of scrawny old alley cats searching for slow rats. A windowless warehouse, secured by a large padlock, was what I found. I tugged the lock — a standard but useless gesture — then scanned the area before returning to the door. A big fat zero.

I jiggled the padlock a second time. Odd place for the jet set to spend a late Saturday night. Good chance this hangout had an inside makeover and wild, expensive parties jammed until early in the A.M. Or maybe a glittering dance floor with pounding music and snazzy bartenders brought this place to life after hours. I could picture Christina in a skintight tank top, her bulging arms flexed to the max, standing at the bar, slamming a shot.

"Hey!" She'd flash me a nod and motion for me to join her.

"Tina, how's it going?" I'd slap her five.

"I wondered if you were going to make it." She high-signed the bartender and pulled out a stool for me. "What's your pleasure?"

"Margarita Gold."

She ordered my drink while I cased the joint. The warehouse had been renovated into an elaborate private nightclub. Music blared, colored lights flashed from a crowded dance floor and an amazing selection of glamour girls packed the room. I scouted for Nikki, but as I had suspected, she was a no show.

"You here alone?" I asked nonchalantly.

Christina leaned in close. Her hand brushed across my ass. "Not anymore." The determination in her slow, suggestive words was crystal clear.

Not anymore. Yeah, this woman was smooth as exotic silk and just as expensive. Her style had Valentino or St. Laurent written all over it. She was smothered in gold — several wide bands on her fingers, a thick-linked bracelet on her wrist. And the Rolex she wore, blue-faced and diamond-loaded, was no trinket.

I kicked around the image of Nikki — at my desk, she was talking about Christina. In and out of fantasyland, she drifted. *I shrugged off my uneasiness about things and went ahead with the loan, in my name only,* she had said. I eyeballed Christina's diamond pinkie ring and buried my distaste. I smelled a rat. No telling what kind of perks came with the package Nikki offered.

"Here." Christina handed me my drink. The flashy Rolex sparkled.

"Nice watch," I said.

"Gift," Christina replied. A no-big-deal tone iced her words.

"Not bad," I said under my breath. *And the rings, the bracelet and the fancy duds, were those gifts, too?*

"You know," Christina said in a low voice, "it's a special kind of woman that deserves gifts."

She slipped the Rolex off and snapped it around my wrist. Before I had a chance to respond, she grabbed my hand and led me through the crowd of perfumed women and into a darkened room off the back corner of the bar.

"Hurry, hurry," Christina muttered, closing the door behind us. She guided me, face down, across a long table and tugged down my pants. Her power-filled hands seized my waist.

"I want to fuck you." Her words were hard. Her hands were fast. She separated my legs with short, quick kicks against my boots. "Atta girl, atta girl."

Bent over, I grasped the table's farthest edge. The Rolex was heavy on my wrist. Even in the darkness, a muffled glint from the diamonds was crystal clear. Why the hell not stretch all the way for her?

Behind me, she fumbled with her own pants. Her breath was loud and hurried. The pants fell to her knees. There was nothing between us until she pressed against me and I felt it. Her hands had returned to my waist and the full, rounded tip of a dildo squeezed eagerly between the cheeks of my ass.

"I packed it all night, just for you. Just so I could fuck you right." Christina leaned in and the rubberized toy inched closer to my asshole.

Fuck me where, exactly? I wanted to ask, but my question was answered before I had a chance to mouth the first word.

"In your ass," she whispered. "With a nice, big butt plug."

The thick, smooth plug tapped against my tiny ass slit. She pulled my cheeks apart and a cold spurt of lube dribbled down my exposed crack.

"Now, baby, now," she moaned as she popped the tip past the restrictive portal.

My body jerked involuntarily. My puckered opening felt stretched to the max. Even though it pinched like hell, a storm of fireworks shot through my canal. A free-for-all of feelings swarmed me like bees. I wanted to pull her out. I needed her to plunge in. I was scared of hurting — yet I craved what lay ahead.

Christina pressed in. Slowly, she slid the plug deeper. I wanted to let her in, but my tight passageway clamped down involuntarily. That didn't stop Christina. She burrowed in farther, forcing the walls to balloon open. *And it was so good.* I spread my legs further and tilted my ass higher. *Go ahead, split me wide.*

Like she had climbed to the top of a water slide and was ready to make her dive, Christina stopped. Without moving the plug, she grabbed my hair and jerked my head back. A sudden case of cold feet hit. What if it hurt when she fucked me like this? What if . . .

Wham, Christina thrust all the way in then stopped again. "Ready, baby?"

My ass felt filled. Every part of me raged with heat. *And it was better than good.*

"Yes," I muttered.

She dragged out unbearably slow and then, like she had pulled back a slingshot, snap, she let go. Into my ready, open, greedy asshole, she pounded. I gripped the table to keep from flying across the room. She moved like a bronco rider while I bucked beneath her. She slapped my cheeks, egging me on. My small tunnel burned and throbbed with bizarre gratification. Sheer lust twisted so tightly with discomfort that it was hard to tell them apart. And she plunged in, dove deep, pushed me to the edge of the world. As close to heaven as one could get; it was Christina who led the way.

I jiggled the padlock one last time, then returned to my car. The crotch of my pants was soaked. Fingernail marks cut into my palms from having clenched my fists so tightly. For a second, I thought I smelled Christina's scent but I waved it out of my way. Not a problem, not anymore. I checked my Timex, thought of the Rolex and smiled. With better things to think about than imaginary fragrances, I headed downtown for some shop-till-drop. Tonight, I needed to dazzle.

"Ever hear of Pleasure Unlimited?" I watched my reflection in the bedroom mirror as I spoke into the phone. The new threads looked good. Dressed like this, I could run with the best.

"Pleasure Unlimited?" Nikki had that far away tone in her voice. "I don't think so."

"You seeing Christina tonight?" I asked, distracted. Damn, if I didn't look great.

"She's out of town until tomorrow, why?"

"Just keeping tabs," I said casually. Maybe I should have updated Nikki about the lead I was following, but I stuffed the info. Seemed like the right move. First, some one-on-one with Christina — best to catch the rat with stolen cheese — before I

161

delivered the dagger that would pierce Nikki's heart. I raised the collar on my new leather coat and checked a side angle of myself. Call me sentimental. Call me soft. I just hate to see a damsel with tears in her eyes.

It was eleven P.M. when I returned to the warehouse. This time the street was lined with fancy cars. A lone woman leaned against the entranceway. She wore thick, black boots and a bulky leather jacket. Wire-rimmed sunglasses were perched on her nose and a cigarette dangled from her mouth.

"Hey, what's happening." I gave her a nod.

The woman pushed herself from the wall, ran her hand through her short, spiked hair and stepped between me and the door. "You got an invitation?" She glared at me over the rim of her glasses.

"Tina." I held my ground. Tough women with bad attitudes got on my nerves.

"Tina?" She gave me a slow onceover.

"Yeah. Tina," I replied. Tough women with bad ears were even worse.

She kicked the door open with her foot. "Go ahead."

Hell of a conversationalist, too. I hoped the rest of the gang were a little more jovial. Past her, I wandered into the dimly lit hallway where two women, their faces hidden behind glitzy masks, were attending the interior door.

"Good evening." A golden mask, elaborately decorated with red and green sequins, was handed to me. "And you're a guest of?"

"Tina" What was this, a masquerade ball?

"And did she tell you the rules?" the other asked.

The rules. Now things were getting interesting. I shook my head.

"Mask stays on. No real names. No drugs. Safe sex only. Any questions?"

Yeah, I thought, one big question. What the hell had I gotten myself into? "Nah," I said, as if I knew the ropes, like I'd been in situations like this a hundred times before. I put the mask on.

"Enjoy yourself." The women stepped aside.

It's times like this that I really missed my smokes. Sure, I had had a brief fantasy or two about jazzing around with Christina. But I'm a pro, I have standards, a rep to uphold. Especially after last summer's foul-up. A husband had suspected his wife of fooling around and had hired me to get the goods. I bellied up with a big zilch. But he was obsessed and kept me on her tail. I was on her ass three solid months before the case finally cracked. One morning, out of the blue, she went straight to the downtown Hilton. In my glory, I snapped photos as she walked into the lobby, more photos as she registered. With each click of the camera, I saw dollar signs. Nothing like a fat bonus for a job well done.

Slip-ups happen. She rented a room then walked right up to me in the goddamn lobby. Lust dripped from her like heat-wave sweat. She handed me a key and smiled — one of those sultry smiles. The next thing I knew, I was the center of a messy love triangle. Took a while for that storm to blow over. I've buried my nose in disability cases from that time on. Until Nikki.

Get caught up in some sex club scandal with a no-bargain woman like Christina? Ruin a chance to further my career with a money-to-burn client like Nikki? No way. One course in that school of hard knocks was enough. I figured I'd check the joint out, get the dope on Christina and get the hell out. I just wished I could have one cig.

"Cigarette?" A tall, topless cigarette girl, laden with a strapped-on tray, was the first to greet me. I peered at her array of cigarettes and candy and then stared hungrily at her pert, pink breasts. Her nipples craned forward like tiny seeds. I fought a strong urge to pluck them.

"Smoking's allowed?" I reluctantly shifted my focus from her divine breasts to her full red lips. One drag was all I needed.

"In the lounge." The woman motioned down a hallway that was crowded with masked women.

I handed her a five, grabbed a pack of smokes and worked my way through the women. I wondered where Christina was. Women stood along the walls. Some were simply talking, others were kissing. As I passed, I could hear soft moans and hard breaths.

"Hey, it's the woman from the gym," someone called from behind me.

I turned, hoping to see Christina, but didn't spot her anywhere. A black-masked woman was squeezing the cigarette girl's thickened, pink nipples — like I could have done, should have done when I had had the chance. Another, pressed against the wall, was writhing passionately as two rhinestone-masked women held her arms high. Across from them, a long-haired blonde, decked in spike heels and leather chaps, leaned against a doorway. She looked me straight in the eye, curled her finger in a come-here gesture and smiled seductively.

Me? I glanced over my shoulder, then back at her. *Me?*

Yes, you.

The woman who was pinned against the wall was getting louder. Her rhinestone-studded captors had started fucking her and sexual energy bounced from the walls. Desire knotted in my clit. The entire place smelled like sex.

I glanced back to the blonde.

Yes, you.

What difference would a ten-minute break make in the scheme of things? I scanned the hall for Christina, who was nowhere to be seen, then pushed my way toward Goldilocks.

"You know me from the gym?" I asked. Her plush breasts, decorated with a strand of thick pearls, spilled from her leather halter. I arm-wrestled a thunderbolt urge to bury my face between the lustrous beads and the fleshy orbs.

She slowly shook her head. The black leather mask she wore struck a hard contrast with her scarlet-painted lips. "Someone knows you from the gym," she said provocatively. "Whereas I know you from that someone." She grabbed my jacket and pulled me, just inches, from her glossy mouth.

"Is she here?" I muttered.

The blonde covered my mouth with her own. Her hands eagerly pushed up my shirt. She kissed me. She scanned my body with rough caresses. Her spicy clove fragrance braided with the scent from my new leather jacket. The mix was lethal. Dizzy with desire, I let her navigate me to a softly lit alcove. A doctor's examination table occupied the otherwise bare space.

There was no argument from me as she pushed me onto the table. Wasting no time, I unhooked her halter. The black leather fell aside and her cocoa-tipped breasts hung, voluptuous and succulent, smack dab above my face.

I grabbed her tits and sucked the large areolas deep into my desperate mouth. She pulled back and her elongated, brown nipples snapped from my mouth. I bobbed to latch back onto the erect stubs but Goldilocks bounced her sweet, puckered tips just out of reach.

Like a cat in heat, I squirmed beneath her. I wanted more. More. A gathering of masked women surrounded the table. They watched her tease, they watched her tempt. A woman ripped at my shirt. Another held down my head. Someone tugged my pants to my ankles.

Goldilocks gave me a shoot-the-moon smile then climbed from the table. The circle split and a woman in black sauntered toward me. With her telltale cocky swagger and her buffed-to-the-max build, I was sure as shit who she was.

"Tina," I said on reflex.

"No names," a woman whispered.

Tina motioned toward Goldilocks's strand of pearls. Goldilocks pulled the pearls over her head, handed them to Tina, and then planted a hot and heavy kiss on her mouth. I could see their tongues tangle. I could hear Tina's want-to-be-fucked moans.

Tina broke from Goldilocks and turned to me. "I bet you'd look nice in pearls." Her voice was slick ice. "It's a special kind of woman who deserves gifts. Right?" She glanced at the blonde.

"Right," the blonde murmured.

"Are *you* a special kind of woman?" Tina's focus shifted from me to the pearls now bunched in her hand. She reached into her pocket and withdrew a bottle of lube. The women murmured as if they knew, all too well, what was coming.

Tina coated the pearls with lube, looped them into a thick knot and spread my legs. The knotted pearls dangled inches from my bulging clit. I arched my hips. I could only imagine how cool, how smooth, the slippery beads would feel against my snatch.

Tina slowly tucked a lone pearl into my cunt. The women cooled their whispers. Egged by her persistent finger, one pearl, then another, tunneled in. One by one, each polished pearl was nudged then burrowed into my throbbing slit.

"Give her the knot," an overanxious observer demanded.

"Yeah," said another.

The knot. An image flashed in my mind — the bulky knot, the thick knot, the cool, bumpy, hard knot being pressed into my aching hole. A buzzing tension not only tightened my pussy, but seemed to ricochet through the entire group. Sex currents bombarded me as if we were all wired together. We were all hurting for more. Way more. *Hurting for the knot.*

Yeah, Tina was a crowd pleaser. She knew how to run a show. Was there ever a question? Was there ever a doubt that Tina couldn't take anybody anywhere. Her biceps were iron. Her triceps were steel. Slicked-back hair, penetrating eyes — she was attitude personified, attitude unleashed. She was every woman's dream, every woman's fantasy — and she was between my legs, filling me with pearls.

Give her the knot. Give her the knot. Words, like a mantra, like a prayer, torpedoed around the room. *The knot. The knot. Yeah, give me the knot.*

Tina would never let me down, *us* down. Never. Slowly, she urged the bulging bundle of pearls until they were sucked well past the portal of my open and ready pussy. In they slipped. Her fingers shoveled the pearls deeper, as deep as possible. I moaned. We all moaned.

A long strand, a full strand — I thought of how sweetly those pearls had brushed against Goldilocks's full breasts — those brown-tipped, luscious, mouth-watering tits. Tina tugged lightly. A slow snap of her wrist and the first few pearls dragged out of my tightened sex groove. Plop. Plop. Pearl after pearl. The sensation made me crazy. My pussy rippled with pleasure. Plop. Plop. With each short yank, the knot slowly traveled closer toward exit.

I clamped down. I wanted to feel every surface, every pearl, every bump as it pressed and prodded against the walls of my cunt. And she pulled. She pulled. She pulled and pulled and pulled. The pressure surged through me. Visions of Goldilocks's breasts, of Tina's thighs, slammed through me. A quick flash of Tina, strong and tough, holding Nikki, fucking Nikki. And Nikki — hot Nikki, classy Nikki — a glamour girl with problems. She was crying on my shoulder, she was buying me gifts. The pearls were jerked and the sensation could have launched torpedoes. I was fucking her, taking her. Nikki. Nikki. Nikki.

"Nikki!" I cried as I came.

"Nikki? Nikki?" Tina yanked me from the table and pushed me through the women. Roughly flung from a sexual stupor, struggling with my pants, I hobbled after her. She pulled me into a small room, locked the door and lifted her mask. "Were you hired by Nikki? Were you?"

Red-faced, I buttoned my shirt and snapped my pants.

She ran her hand across her firm breasts and glared into my face. "Goddamn Nikki and her neurotic ploys. Did you think you're the first she's hired to check me out?"

I kept my trap shut and opted to keep tabs on the sparks in Christina's eyes instead. Her stance was tense. Her entire body was flexed and ready. The room, filled only with the powerful image of Christina, seemed suddenly even smaller.

"And are you fucking her?" Christina sneered. "That's what gets her off. The attention, the damsel-in-distress bit. Starting this sex club wasn't enough to satisfy her yearnings. No. Nikki hires P.I.s for *her* kicks." Christina stepped closer. "But you liked me, didn't you?" She pushed me against the cool wall. "*Didn't you?*" That wild, intoxicating scent — *the way she smells when she has sex* — filled me.

Trying to keep my cool, I took a deep breath. "No, I'm not fucking her," I said carefully, lifting my mask. "And yes, I liked you."

* * * * *

Christ, Nikki had really put poor Christina through the wringer with her shenanigans. Dropping Nikki like a hot potato was the best move Christina's made in a long time.

Christina and I have started our own business. Sure, I had to put up a pretty penny, put my neck on the line, but Christina says we'll be looking at a good profit soon enough. I sold the equipment from my P.I. business and reinvested with Christina. Well, actually, I came up with the capital, seeing that she's temporarily short on cash. It seems her long lost mother left her some big bucks, but it's tied up in probate. And lately, Christina's been so stressed out . . .

Regardless, I love Christina. She dazzles. She has charisma. She's impossible to resist.

A few of the publications of
THE NAIAD PRESS, INC.
P.O. Box 10543 • **Tallahassee, Florida 32302**
Phone (904) 539-5965
Toll-Free Order Number: 1-800-533-1973
Mail orders welcome. Please include 15% postage.
Write or call for our free catalog which also features an
incredible selection of lesbian videos.

COSTA BRAVA by Marta Balletbo Coll. 144 pp. Read the book,
see the movie! ISBN 1-56280-153-8 $11.95

MEETING MAGDALENE & OTHER STORIES by
Marilyn Freeman. 160 pp. Read the book, see the movie!
ISBN 1-56280-170-8 11.95

SECOND FIDDLE by Kate Calloway. 240 pp. P.I. Cassidy James'
second case. ISBN 1-56280-169-6 11.95

LAUREL by Isabel Miller. 128 pp. By the author of the beloved
Patience and Sarah. ISBN 1-56280-146-5 10.95

LOVE OR MONEY by Jackie Calhoun. 240 pp. The romance of
real life. ISBN 1-56280-147-3 10.95

SMOKE AND MIRRORS by Pat Welch. 224 pp. 5th Helen Black
Mystery. ISBN 1-56280-143-0 10.95

DANCING IN THE DARK edited by Barbara Grier & Christine
Cassidy. 272 pp. Erotic love stories by Naiad Press authors.
ISBN 1-56280-144-9 14.95

TIME AND TIME AGAIN by Catherine Ennis. 176 pp. Passionate
love affair. ISBN 1-56280-145-7 10.95

PAXTON COURT by Diane Salvatore. 256 pp. Erotic and wickedly
funny contemporary tale about the business of learning to live
together. ISBN 1-56280-114-7 10.95

INNER CIRCLE by Claire McNab. 208 pp. 8th Carol Ashton
Mystery. ISBN 1-56280-135-X 10.95

LESBIAN SEX: AN ORAL HISTORY by Susan Johnson.
240 pp. Need we say more? ISBN 1-56280-142-2 14.95

BABY, IT'S COLD by Jaye Maiman. 256 pp. 5th Robin Miller
Mystery. ISBN 1-56280-141-4 19.95

WILD THINGS by Karin Kallmaker. 240 pp. By the undisputed
mistress of lesbian romance. ISBN 1-56280-139-2 10.95

BAR GIRLS by Lauran Hoffman. 176 pp. See the movie, read the book! ISBN 1-56280-115-5   10.95

THE FIRST TIME EVER edited by Barbara Grier & Christine Cassidy. 272 pp. Love stories by Naiad Press authors.
ISBN 1-56280-086-8   14.95

MISS PETTIBONE AND MISS McGRAW by Brenda Weathers. 208 pp. A charming ghostly love story. ISBN 1-56280-151-1   10.95

CHANGES by Jackie Calhoun. 208 pp. Involved romance and relationships. ISBN 1-56280-083-3   10.95

FAIR PLAY by Rose Beecham. 256 pp. 3rd Amanda Valentine Mystery. ISBN 1-56280-081-7   10.95

PAYBACK by Celia Cohen. 176 pp. A gripping thriller of romance, revenge and betrayal. ISBN 1-56280-084-1   10.95

THE BEACH AFFAIR by Barbara Johnson. 224 pp. Sizzling summer romance/mystery/intrigue. ISBN 1-56280-090-6   10.95

GETTING THERE by Robbi Sommers. 192 pp. Nobody does it like Robbi! ISBN 1-56280-099-X   10.95

FINAL CUT by Lisa Haddock. 208 pp. 2nd Carmen Ramirez Mystery. ISBN 1-56280-088-4   10.95

FLASHPOINT by Katherine V. Forrest. 256 pp. A Lesbian blockbuster! ISBN 1-56280-079-5   10.95

CLAIRE OF THE MOON by Nicole Conn. Audio Book —Read by Marianne Hyatt. ISBN 1-56280-113-9   16.95

FOR LOVE AND FOR LIFE: INTIMATE PORTRAITS OF LESBIAN COUPLES by Susan Johnson. 224 pp.
ISBN 1-56280-091-4   14.95

DEVOTION by Mindy Kaplan. 192 pp. See the movie — read the book! ISBN 1-56280-093-0   10.95

SOMEONE TO WATCH by Jaye Maiman. 272 pp. 4th Robin Miller Mystery. ISBN 1-56280-095-7   10.95

GREENER THAN GRASS by Jennifer Fulton. 208 pp. A young woman — a stranger in her bed. ISBN 1-56280-092-2   10.95

TRAVELS WITH DIANA HUNTER by Regine Sands. Erotic lesbian romp. Audio Book (2 cassettes) ISBN 1-56280-107-4   16.95

CABIN FEVER by Carol Schmidt. 256 pp. Sizzling suspense and passion. ISBN 1-56280-089-1   10.95

THERE WILL BE NO GOODBYES by Laura DeHart Young. 192 pp. Romantic love, strength, and friendship. ISBN 1-56280-103-1   10.95

FAULTLINE by Sheila Ortiz Taylor. 144 pp. Joyous comic lesbian novel. ISBN 1-56280-108-2   9.95

OPEN HOUSE by Pat Welch. 176 pp. 4th Helen Black Mystery.
ISBN 1-56280-102-3   10.95

ONCE MORE WITH FEELING by Peggy J. Herring. 240 pp. Lighthearted, loving romantic adventure. ISBN 1-56280-089-2   10.95

FOREVER by Evelyn Kennedy. 224 pp. Passionate romance — love overcoming all obstacles. ISBN 1-56280-094-9   10.95

WHISPERS by Kris Bruyer. 176 pp. Romantic ghost story ISBN 1-56280-082-5   10.95

NIGHT SONGS by Penny Mickelbury. 224 pp. 2nd Gianna Maglione Mystery. ISBN 1-56280-097-3   10.95

GETTING TO THE POINT by Teresa Stores. 256 pp. Classic southern Lesbian novel. ISBN 1-56280-100-7   10.95

PAINTED MOON by Karin Kallmaker. 224 pp. Delicious Kallmaker romance. ISBN 1-56280-075-2   10.95

THE MYSTERIOUS NAIAD edited by Katherine V. Forrest & Barbara Grier. 320 pp. Love stories by Naiad Press authors. ISBN 1-56280-074-4   14.95

DAUGHTERS OF A CORAL DAWN by Katherine V. Forrest. 240 pp. Tenth Anniversay Edition. ISBN 1-56280-104-X   10.95

BODY GUARD by Claire McNab. 208 pp. 6th Carol Ashton Mystery. ISBN 1-56280-073-6   10.95

CACTUS LOVE by Lee Lynch. 192 pp. Stories by the beloved storyteller. ISBN 1-56280-071-X   9.95

SECOND GUESS by Rose Beecham. 216 pp. 2nd Amanda Valentine Mystery. ISBN 1-56280-069-8   9.95

A RAGE OF MAIDENS by Lauren Wright Douglas. 240 pp. 6th Caitlin Reece Mystery. ISBN 1-56280-068-X   10.95

TRIPLE EXPOSURE by Jackie Calhoun. 224 pp. Romantic drama involving many characters. ISBN 1-56280-067-1   10.95

UP, UP AND AWAY by Catherine Ennis. 192 pp. Delightful romance. ISBN 1-56280-065-5   9.95

PERSONAL ADS by Robbi Sommers. 176 pp. Sizzling short stories. ISBN 1-56280-059-0   10.95

CROSSWORDS by Penny Sumner. 256 pp. 2nd Victoria Cross Mystery. ISBN 1-56280-064-7   9.95

SWEET CHERRY WINE by Carol Schmidt. 224 pp. A novel of suspense. ISBN 1-56280-063-9   9.95

CERTAIN SMILES by Dorothy Tell. 160 pp. Erotic short stories. ISBN 1-56280-066-3   9.95

EDITED OUT by Lisa Haddock. 224 pp. 1st Carmen Ramirez Mystery. ISBN 1-56280-077-9   9.95

WEDNESDAY NIGHTS by Camarin Grae. 288 pp. Sexy adventure. ISBN 1-56280-060-4   10.95

SMOKEY O by Celia Cohen. 176 pp. Relationships on the
playing field. ISBN 1-56280-057-4   9.95

KATHLEEN O'DONALD by Penny Hayes. 256 pp. Rose and
Kathleen find each other and employment in 1909 NYC.
ISBN 1-56280-070-1   9.95

STAYING HOME by Elisabeth Nonas. 256 pp. Molly and Alix
want a baby . . . or do they? ISBN 1-56280-076-0   10.95

TRUE LOVE by Jennifer Fulton. 240 pp. Six lesbians searching
for love in all the "right" places. ISBN 1-56280-035-3   10.95

KEEPING SECRETS by Penny Mickelbury. 208 pp. 1st Gianna
Maglione Mystery. ISBN 1-56280-052-3   9.95

THE ROMANTIC NAIAD edited by Katherine V. Forrest &
Barbara Grier. 336 pp. Love stories by Naiad Press authors.
ISBN 1-56280-054-X   14.95

UNDER MY SKIN by Jaye Maiman. 336 pp. 3rd Robin Miller
Mystery. ISBN 1-56280-049-3.   10.95

CAR POOL by Karin Kallmaker. 272pp. Lesbians on wheels
and then some! ISBN 1-56280-048-5   10.95

NOT TELLING MOTHER: STORIES FROM A LIFE by Diane
Salvatore. 176 pp. Her 3rd novel. ISBN 1-56280-044-2   9.95

GOBLIN MARKET by Lauren Wright Douglas. 240pp. 5th Caitlin
Reece Mystery. ISBN 1-56280-047-7   10.95

LONG GOODBYES by Nikki Baker. 256 pp. 3rd Virginia Kelly
Mystery. ISBN 1-56280-042-6   9.95

FRIENDS AND LOVERS by Jackie Calhoun. 224 pp. Mid-
western Lesbian lives and loves. ISBN 1-56280-041-8   10.95

THE CAT CAME BACK by Hilary Mullins. 208 pp. Highly
praised Lesbian novel. ISBN 1-56280-040-X   9.95

BEHIND CLOSED DOORS by Robbi Sommers. 192 pp. Hot,
erotic short stories. ISBN 1-56280-039-6   9.95

CLAIRE OF THE MOON by Nicole Conn. 192 pp. See the
movie — read the book! ISBN 1-56280-038-8   10.95

SILENT HEART by Claire McNab. 192 pp. Exotic Lesbian
romance. ISBN 1-56280-036-1   10.95

THE SPY IN QUESTION by Amanda Kyle Williams. 256 pp.
4th Madison McGuire Mystery. ISBN 1-56280-037-X   9.95

SAVING GRACE by Jennifer Fulton. 240 pp. Adventure and
romantic entanglement. ISBN 1-56280-051-5   10.95

CURIOUS WINE by Katherine V. Forrest. 176 pp. Tenth Anniver-
sary Edition. The most popular contemporary Lesbian love story.
ISBN 1-56280-053-1   10.95
    Audio Book (2 cassettes)   ISBN 1-56280-105-8   16.95

THE END OF APRIL by Penny Sumner. 240 pp. 1st Victoria
Cross Mystery. ISBN 1-56280-007-8   8.95

KISS AND TELL by Robbi Sommers. 192 pp. Scorching stories
by the author of *Pleasures.* ISBN 1-56280-005-1   10.95

STILL WATERS by Pat Welch. 208 pp. 2nd Helen Black Mystery.
ISBN 0-941483-97-5   9.95

TO LOVE AGAIN by Evelyn Kennedy. 208 pp. Wildly romantic
love story. ISBN 0-941483-85-1   9.95

IN THE GAME by Nikki Baker. 192 pp. 1st Virginia Kelly
Mystery. ISBN 1-56280-004-3   9.95

STRANDED by Camarin Grae. 320 pp. Entertaining, riveting
adventure. ISBN 0-941483-99-1   9.95

THE DAUGHTERS OF ARTEMIS by Lauren Wright Douglas.
240 pp. 3rd Caitlin Reece Mystery. ISBN 0-941483-95-9   9.95

CLEARWATER by Catherine Ennis. 176 pp. Romantic secrets
of a small Louisiana town. ISBN 0-941483-65-7   8.95

THE HALLELUJAH MURDERS by Dorothy Tell. 176 pp. 2nd
Poppy Dillworth Mystery. ISBN 0-941483-88-6   8.95

SECOND CHANCE by Jackie Calhoun. 256 pp. Contemporary
Lesbian lives and loves. ISBN 0-941483-93-2   9.95

BENEDICTION by Diane Salvatore. 272 pp. Striking, contemporary romantic novel. ISBN 0-941483-90-8   10.95

TOUCHWOOD by Karin Kallmaker. 240 pp. Loving, May/
December romance. ISBN 0-941483-76-2   9.95

COP OUT by Claire McNab. 208 pp. 4th Carol Ashton Mystery.
ISBN 0-941483-84-3   10.95

THE BEVERLY MALIBU by Katherine V. Forrest. 288 pp. 3rd
Kate Delafield Mystery. ISBN 0-941483-48-7   11.95

THE PROVIDENCE FILE by Amanda Kyle Williams. 256 pp.
2nd Madison McGuire Mystery. ISBN 0-941483-92-4   8.95

I LEFT MY HEART by Jaye Maiman. 320 pp. 1st Robin Miller
Mystery. ISBN 0-941483-72-X   10.95

THE PRICE OF SALT by Patricia Highsmith (writing as Claire
Morgan). 288 pp. Classic lesbian novel, first issued in 1952 . . .
acknowledged by its author under her own, very famous, name.
ISBN 1-56280-003-5   10.95

SIDE BY SIDE by Isabel Miller. 256 pp. From beloved author of
Patience and Sarah. ISBN 0-941483-77-0   10.95

STAYING POWER: LONG TERM LESBIAN COUPLES by
Susan E. Johnson. 352 pp. Joys of coupledom. ISBN 0-941-483-75-4   14.95

SLICK by Camarin Grae. 304 pp. Exotic, erotic adventure.
ISBN 0-941483-74-6   9.95

SOUTH OF THE LINE by Catherine Ennis. 216 pp. Civil War
adventure. ISBN 0-941483-29-0   8.95

WOMAN PLUS WOMAN by Dolores Klaich. 300 pp. Supurb
Lesbian overview. ISBN 0-941483-28-2   9.95

THE FINER GRAIN by Denise Ohio. 216 pp. Brilliant young
college lesbian novel. ISBN 0-941483-11-8   8.95

BEFORE STONEWALL: THE MAKING OF A GAY AND
LESBIAN COMMUNITY by Andrea Weiss & Greta Schiller.
96 pp., 25 illus. ISBN 0-941483-20-7   7.95

OSTEN'S BAY by Zenobia N. Vole. 204 pp. Sizzling adventure
romance set on Bonaire. ISBN 0-941483-15-0   8.95

LESSONS IN MURDER by Claire McNab. 216 pp. 1st Carol Ashton
Mystery. ISBN 0-941483-14-2   10.95

YELLOWTHROAT by Penny Hayes. 240 pp. Margarita, bandit,
kidnaps Julia. ISBN 0-941483-10-X   8.95

SAPPHISTRY: THE BOOK OF LESBIAN SEXUALITY by
Pat Califia. 3d edition, revised. 208 pp. ISBN 0-941483-24-X   10.95

CHERISHED LOVE by Evelyn Kennedy. 192 pp. Erotic Lesbian
love story. ISBN 0-941483-08-8   10.95

THE SECRET IN THE BIRD by Camarin Grae. 312 pp. Striking,
psychological suspense novel. ISBN 0-941483-05-3   8.95

TO THE LIGHTNING by Catherine Ennis. 208 pp. Romantic
Lesbian 'Robinson Crusoe' adventure. ISBN 0-941483-06-1   8.95

DREAMS AND SWORDS by Katherine V. Forrest. 192 pp.
Romantic, erotic, imaginative stories. ISBN 0-941483-03-7   10.95

MEMORY BOARD by Jane Rule. 336 pp. Memorable novel
about an aging Lesbian couple. ISBN 0-941483-02-9   12.95

THE ALWAYS ANONYMOUS BEAST by Lauren Wright Douglas.
224 pp. 1st Caitlin Reece Mystery.
ISBN 0-941483-04-5   8.95

MURDER AT THE NIGHTWOOD BAR by Katherine V. Forrest.
240 pp. 2nd Kate Delafield Mystery. ISBN 0-930044-92-4   11.95

WINGED DANCER by Camarin Grae. 228 pp. Erotic Lesbian
adventure story. ISBN 0-930044-88-6   8.95

PAZ by Camarin Grae. 336 pp. Romantic Lesbian adventurer
with the power to change the world. ISBN 0-930044-89-4   8.95

SOUL SNATCHER by Camarin Grae. 224 pp. A puzzle, an
adventure, a mystery — Lesbian romance. ISBN 0-930044-90-8   8.95

THE LOVE OF GOOD WOMEN by Isabel Miller. 224 pp.
Long-awaited new novel by the author of the beloved *Patience
and Sarah*. ISBN 0-930044-81-9   8.95

THE LONG TRAIL by Penny Hayes. 248 pp. Vivid adventures
of two women in love in the old west. ISBN 0-930044-76-2 8.95

AN EMERGENCE OF GREEN by Katherine V. Forrest. 288
pp. Powerful novel of sexual discovery. ISBN 0-930044-69-X 11.95

THE LESBIAN PERIODICALS INDEX edited by Claire Potter.
432 pp. Author & subject index. ISBN 0-930044-74-6 12.95

DESERT OF THE HEART by Jane Rule. 224 pp. A classic;
basis for the movie *Desert Hearts*. ISBN 0-930044-73-8 10.95

SEX VARIANT WOMEN IN LITERATURE by Jeannette
Howard Foster. 448 pp. Literary history. ISBN 0-930044-65-7 8.95

A HOT-EYED MODERATE by Jane Rule. 252 pp. Hard-hitting
essays on gay life; writing; art. ISBN 0-930044-57-6 7.95

AMATEUR CITY by Katherine V. Forrest. 224 pp. 1st Kate
Delafield Mystery. ISBN 0-930044-55-X 10.95

THE SOPHIE HOROWITZ STORY by Sarah Schulman. 176 pp.
Engaging novel of madcap intrigue. ISBN 0-930044-54-1 7.95

THE YOUNG IN ONE ANOTHER'S ARMS by Jane Rule.
224 pp. Classic Jane Rule. ISBN 0-930044-53-3 9.95

AGAINST THE SEASON by Jane Rule. 224 pp. Luminous,
complex novel of interrelationships. ISBN 0-930044-48-7 8.95

LOVERS IN THE PRESENT AFTERNOON by Kathleen Fleming.
288 pp. A novel about recovery and growth. ISBN 0-930044-46-0 8.95

CONTRACT WITH THE WORLD by Jane Rule. 340 pp. Powerful, panoramic novel of gay life. ISBN 0-930044-28-2 9.95

THIS IS NOT FOR YOU by Jane Rule. 284 pp. A letter to a
beloved is also an intricate novel. ISBN 0-930044-25-8 8.95

OUTLANDER by Jane Rule. 207 pp. Short stories and essays by
one of our finest writers. ISBN 0-930044-17-7 8.95

These are just a few of the many Naiad Press titles — we are the oldest and
largest lesbian/feminist publishing company in the world. We also offer an
enormous selection of lesbian video products. Please request a complete
catalog. We offer personal service; we encourage and welcome direct mail
orders from individuals who have limited access to bookstores carrying our
publications.